Roy Thomas presents
THE HEAP
Volume ONE

FIRST EDITION
NOVEMBER 2012

Bookshop ISBN 978-1-84863-463-3
Slipcase ISBN 978-1-84863-464-0

Published by
PS Artbooks Ltd.
www.psartbooks.co.uk

A subsidary of PS Publishing Ltd.
www.pspublishing.co.uk
award-winning, UK-based, independent publisher of SF, fantasy, horror, crime & more...

Copyright © PS Artbooks 2012

HEAP OF THANKS:
The Publishers would like to thank the following, without whose help this project would have been
considerably more difficult than it ended up . . .
Barry Pearl, Bob Bailey and Mike DeLisa.
Additional images kindly supplied by Heritage Auction Galleries http://www.ha.com/c/index.zx

Originally published in magazine form by Hillman Periodicals, Inc

Foreword © Roy Thomas 2012
Front Cover color artwork © Mike Ploog 2012
Back Cover drawing of The Heap and Roy Thomas also © Mike Ploog 2012
Endpaper artwork by Ernest Schroeder

Printed in China

design ⌒ communique

· ROY THOMAS · PRESENTS ·

THE HEAP

VOLUME ONE • COLLECTED WORKS

**With a Personal and Historical Introduction
by Roy Thomas**

PS ARTBOOKS

Every once in a while, an opportunity comes along to do something you've been wanting to do for a long time--whether you quite realized it or not. So when Pete and Paul and the rest of the guys at PS Artbooks invited me to become "series consultant" on a projected series (what else?) of quality hardcover collections of classic Golden Age material, I jumped at the chance. Suggesting a complete collection of the 1940s-1950s Heap stories and helping to put it together has been the culmination of a long-time dream... and hopefully not the last one we'll achieve together.

Author/editor Lin Carter used to say, "You write the books you want to read." My own personal corollary: And if you can't write them because they're already written and drawn... then you edit them.

Way to go, guys!

Roy

A Personal *and* Historical Introduction

HEAPING

Roy Thomas has been a writer and editor in the comics field since 1965, mostly for Marvel and DC. Among his favorite mags to script have been All-Star Squadron, Conan the Barbarian, The Savage Sword of Conan, The Avengers, The Invaders, *and* Sub-Mariner. He has received numerous awards for his writing and editing, and in 2000 a Comics Buyer's Guide *poll of professionals and fans named him the field's 4th-favorite writer of the 20th century, and the 5th-favorite editor. He has written several books about comics, with others currently in the works. He also co-wrote two 1980s films,* Conan the Destroyer *and* Fire and Ice. *Roy currently edits the Eisner-winning comics-history magazine* Alter Ego, *works with Stan Lee on the* Spider-Man *newspaper strip, and still scripts the occasional comic, besides serving as series consultant to PS Artbooks on its comics reprint volumes.*

In 2011 he was elected to the Eisner Hall of Fame.

(Above:) Fred Kida's cover for Airboy Comics, Vol. 3, #9 (Oct. 1946), heralded the debut of the Heap's solo feature. In time the ol' Heapster would rival even Airboy and his fabulous Birdplane (nicknamed "Birdie") in popularity.

by Roy Thomas

IT ON

(Above:) The Heap, as drawn by Ernie Schroeder, would be showcased on the cover of several issues of Airboy Comics, *including this one for Vol. 9, #5 (June 1952), where he fights a different sort of swamp creature.*

I. A Heap o' Heaps

Most people reading this preface—I suspect, like, 95% or more—came to the Heap backward.

What I mean is, they probably first read comics like DC's *Swamp Thing* or Marvel's *Man-Thing*—or the earlier Glob in *The Incredible Hulk*—or even Skywald's early-'70s Heap, or Eclipse's Heap revival of the '80s—and only later came to realize there'd been a Heap sloshing around four-color marshes as far back as 1942.

Having been born in 1940, I experienced the original swamp-man-thing the first time around, beginning in the last half of that decade. In the late '40s, though, my main reason for buying a copy of Hillman Periodicals' *Airboy Comics*, the monthly mag in which the Heap appeared, was—Airboy. That blond young aviator with the quasi-costume and the eerily birdlike plane. I have vague memories of the adult pilot-adventurer called Sky Wolf, too, so I must've seen at least one issue of *Airboy* in 1946. I loved his dramatic wolf's-head helmet, but he was really just a fast-fading holdover from the days when the mag had been titled *Air Fighters Comics*. I have a vague feeling that as a kid I did stumble upon the early-'46 Sky Wolf yarn reprinted in this volume, which featured the Heap just before he (it?) lurched off into his/its own series.

Over the next few years through the Feb. 1953 issue, after which *Airboy Comics* was discontinued, I became increasingly intrigued by the Heap stories therein. Flashbacks and captions revealed that, back during the First World War, a German fighter pilot named Baron Eric von Emmelman had crashed and sunk, plane and all, in a swamp in Poland. Mud, muck, and vegetation had slowly transformed him, alive yet not alive, into a monstrosity that now shambled about, mute and near-mindless, always encountering conflicts and somehow always winding up on the right side, which his strength made the *winning* side.

I was a bit puzzled by the Heap. Was he a super-hero, just an unusual (and hideous) one? Or was he part of the burgeoning horror trend in comics, which mostly I failed to appreciate at the time? Or, since the deeds of criminals often dominated the tales, with the Heap just slogging in near story's end to settle someone's hash, was his series more closely related to "true crime" comics, which I likewise loathed?

It slowly dawned on me that the Heap was a *hybrid*—a continuing character with super-hero-level strength (if a distinctly fogbound brain and an inhuman appearance) and even a "secret identity" of sorts in his past, who often ventured into the weeds of crime drama—and, increasingly, into horror fare.

I also sensed an odd similarity between the Heap and another, *slightly* more humanoid entity I'd first encountered in 1946, in the pages of my all-time favorite title, DC's *All-Star Comics*, battling the Justice Society of America. That marshland monster's name was Solomon Grundy—taken, incongruously, from an old nursery rhyme—and he'd first popped up in *All-American Comics* #61 (Oct. 1944), fighting the original Green Lantern. Grundy, too, had once been a human being, a miser who'd perished in so-called Slaughter Swamp; much like the Heap, he'd returned in a perverted distortion of life. Grundy was basically half Heap—though capable of crude speech—yet owed more of his visual aspect to Boris Karloff's (and makeup man Jack Pierce's) Frankenstein Monster in 1930s/40s Universal films. Grundy was similarly lacking in color, as if he'd just stepped out of a black-&-white movie scene, visualized originally by artist Paul Reinman. The writer of the first Green Lantern/Grundy story was Alfrerd Bester, later a highly respected science-fiction author.

Actually, there was a *second* Heap-related character, as well, in those days, though it was a one-shot. Its name was... the Heap.

In the four-color *Mad* #5 (cover-dated June-July 1953, only a few months after the demise of *Airboy Comics*), editor/writer/layout artist Harvey Kurtzman and finishing artist Bill Elder produced "Outer Sanctum!," a parody of a radio suspense series. In it, a mad scientist who lives in the middle of a swamp (yes! again!), stirs up a gumbo which is "a mixture of this swamp," in an attempt to create life. Convinced he's failed, he dumps his brew out of his shack window, where it mingles with swamp-water to form "a festering mish-mosh"—and come to life. As per the caption floating above the first drawing of the very Hillman-Heap-like newborn creature, it **"GREW! STOOD UP! ERECT! A HORRIBLE STANDING GLOB OF SWAMP THING! There was nothing to call it but... HEAP!"** In the next panel, the scientist woke up and "found *IT!*... 'HEAP,' standing outside his door...."

The two preceding captions really cover all the bases, don't they? Except for "Man-Thing," they include every name I dropped in the second paragraph of this introduction—plus a pronoun related to all of them: "Glob"... "Swamp Thing"... "Heap"... and "It" (we'll get to that last one in a minute). While I'm not aware that anyone who knew Kurtzman—including myself—ever asked him about the matter, the "Outer Sanctum!" tale suggests its author was familiar with Hillman's Heap. But we'll probably never know.

(Above:) Solomon Grundy, DC Comics' original muck-monster, was introduced in the Green Lantern story in All-American Comics #61 (Oct. 1944) and would battle GL three more times, including once even taking on the entire Justice Society of America. Script by Alfred Bester, art by Paul Reinman.

(Left:) This panel from Mad #5 (June-July 1953) introduced EC's one-shot Heap in the story "Outer Sanctum!" Script & layout by Harvey Kurtzman, finished art by Bill Elder. [© 2012 EC Publications.]

So what, I wondered, was the connection between Solomon Grundy and these two Heaps? Or *was* there one? Was it only a coincidence that all three of those unappetizing entities originated in a swamp, two of them because of putrid matter forming around a core of a long-dead man?

As it turned out… it probably wasn't.

My first hint of the "secret origins" of the Hillman Heap came in the Nov. 1960 issue (#2) of the science-fiction fanzine *Xero*, which I saw the following February—eight years after the final issue of *Airboy*. In an attempt to recruit writers for the mag's iconic comic-book nostalgia series "All in Color for a Dime," co-editor/publisher Dick Lupoff wrote as an aside to a fan-friend:

"(Dick Schultz, research The Heap, willya? Check it back to its source, Sturgeon's 'It' in the August '40 *Unknown*… it's been reprinted, though I don't recall where just offhand)…."

I knew, even at age twenty, that "Sturgeon" must be noted writer Theodore Sturgeon, author of *More Than Human* and other well-regarded works of science-fiction and fantasy. *Unknown*, I quickly learned, had been a fantasy pulp magazine. That Schultz guy never did write about the Heap for *Xero*, nor did anyone else… but sometime in the next few years, I got hold of a paperback anthology that included the story "It"—and it was a real revelation, beginning with its creepy yet poetic opening paragraphs:

It walked in the woods.

It was never born. It existed. Under the pine needles the fires burn, deep and smokeless in the mold. In heat and in darkness and decay there is growth. There is life and there is growth. It grew, but it was not alive. It walked unbreathing through the woods, and thought and saw and was hideous and strong, and it was not born and it did not live. It grew and moved about without living….

It had no mercy, no laughter, no beauty. It had strength and great intelligence. And—perhaps it could not be destroyed. It crawled out of its mound in the wood and lay pulsing in the sunlight for a long moment. Patches of it shone wetly in the golden glow, parts of it were nubbled and flaked. And whose dead bones had given it the form of a man?

[© 2012 Estate of Theodore Sturgeon.]

In the course of the story's 28 pages, "it" first destroys a young sapling, then a "fear-frozen field creature," crushing the life from them out of an inarticulate curiosity. When attacked by a dog, it kills the beast, then "sat down beside him and began to tear him apart"—again, simply out of curiosity. An adult man soon shares that fate—and a young girl called Babe nearly does—before the creature wanders absently into a stream, which slowly begins to pick its constituent pieces apart, while the monster casually and without alarm observes itself getting smaller… ever smaller. In the end, everything of the creature is washed away by the running water except the human skeleton around which the life-that-was-not-life had formed. Those bones, as snippets of conversation in the middle of the story make clear, were those of a man who'd disappeared years earlier, sinking into the forest floor whose "hot molds" had formed around his skeleton so that there had emerged—a monster.

It seemed likely to me that someone—possibly *two* or even *three* someones—had read this acclaimed short story circa 1940 and, two and four and thirteen years later, respectively, had all coincidentally substituted swamplands for forest, and had generated first the Heap, then Solomon Grundy, then another Heap. But that's only a likelihood—not a certainty.

(Above:) Cover of original 1961 Ballantine edition of Not without Sorcery *by Theodore Sturgeon. This collection reprinted Theodore's Sturgeon's short story "It." Cover artist unknown.*

(Main picture below:) Jack Kirby-pencilled cover for Timely/Marvel's Journey into Mystery #72 (Sept. 1961) introduced the gargantuan Glob. Inker uncertain.

*(Right top:) Kirby pencilled the covers of Strange Tales #82 (March 1961), which featured his and Stan Lee's own monster known only as "It" -
(Right middle:) and of Fantastic Four #1 (Nov. 1961), which introduced the Thing, the first true "super-hero monster." Created by Stan Lee & Jack Kirby; inker unknown.
(Right bottom:) Herb Trimpe drew this cover (and the story inside) for The Incredible Hulk #121 (Nov. 1969), the debut of the Heap-inspired Glob.
The story inside was scripted by Roy Thomas.*

II. The Heap of Things to Come

Over the years, other "It"- or Heap-like entities reared their murky heads in comic books, most prolifically in late-'50s/early-'60s yarns scripted or at least plotted by Timely (pre-Marvel) Comics editor Stan Lee and penciled by the masterful Jack Kirby, formerly of the illustrious Simon & Kirby team that had created Captain America and romance comics. These grotesques, whose various origins owed either much or little or nothing to anything by Sturgeon or Hillman Periodicals, sported names like Monstro, Bruttu, Sporr, Goom, the Glob, Taboo ("The Thing from the Murky Swamp"), and even just plain "It." Several of them did indeed come stalking out of the marshes— and one, an alien called Groot who was quite literally a tree, stomped out of a forest, à la Sturgeon—while others dropped in from outer space or a scientist's lab. But each of them merely rampaged around for a few pages and was destroyed by story's end, and few ever made a second appearance. (Well, the alien Goom was followed by Googam, Son of Goom… but that was less a "return" than an unsuccessful attempt to establish a dynasty.)

This is the point at which, all blushing and blemishes, I myself enter the story… no longer primarily as a reader, but as an active participant.

In 1969, after four years as a writer and associate editor for Marvel Comics, I was tapped by Stan Lee to follow him as scripter of *The Incredible Hulk*. After providing dialogue to a tale plotted by Stan and artist Herb Trimpe, I was left pretty much on my own as to where to go with the series. Stan figured I would know what to do.

The very first thing I did was swipe the Heap.

To my mind, there was already a little something of the Heap in the Hulk—even more so in the ever-lovin', blue-eyed Thing from Marvel's earlier flagship title *Fantastic Four*. Neither of those characters, however, was a rip-off of the Heap (let alone of "It"), even though Stan, who co-created both, has publicly professed to having admired the Hillman character. I'm unaware of Jack Kirby ever mentioning either earlier monster, but he may have.

So the initial *Hulk* story I plotted with Herb Trimpe (#121, cover-dated Nov. 1969) had Bruce Banner's socially challenged alter ego punting several cans of radioactive waste (what else?) into the Florida Everglades, where they and the swamp and a fleeing prison inmate combined into a very Heap-like concoction I christened—The Shape! To Stan, however, the word "shape" implied "female," pure and simple, so he insisted I alter the entity's name to—the Glob. This was merely a re-use of a name from those Lee-Kirby monster mini-epics; but in retrospect, I think he was dead right. The Glob was a hit with the readers, and I brought him back just a few issues later. Other writers have utilized him since.

A year or so after the Glob's debut, I took part in a second Heap-related outbreak. Production manager Sol Brodsky left Marvel to co-found his own smaller comics company, becoming the "Sky" in "Skywald." Over lunch one day soon afterward, Sol was picking my brain for ideas; and, being fond of Sol, I suggested he revive the Heap. Thus, the second issue of Skywald's black-&-white horror comic *Psycho* (March 1971) introduced a brand new permutation of the Heap, with story by Charles McNaughton and art by Ross Andru & Mike Esposito. He, like the original muckmaker, was a pilot—albeit a contemporary one—who crashed his cropduster plane into a tank full of liquid nerve gas and became a brute (complete with fangs like the earliest Hillman version); he retained his human intelligence, however, and was afterwards motivated either to cure or kill himself. After several appearances in *Psycho*, he got his own color comic for one issue, right before Skywald itself crashed and burned.

I was soon involved in a *third* quasi-Heap, as well. For the first issue of Marvel's non-Comics Code b&w comic *Savage Tales*, Stan decided to launch a series about a being he dubbed the Man-Thing. He gave me a sentence or two towards an origin: a young scientist is beset by spies, and a mixture of chemicals and a swamp turns him into a nigh-shapeless monster. Stan never referred to the Heap, but I felt that was what he had at least in the back of his mind. I didn't mind that this new guy would undercut the Glob, but I was less than wild about the name "Man-Thing," since we already had a "Thing" who was a grotesque monstrosity. But I dutifully typed out a full origin plot, expanding on what Stan had given me.

I turned the synopsis over to young Marvel writer Gerry Conway, who fleshed it out into a full script. Illustrator Gray Morrow made the Man-Thing both Heap-like and at the same time a bit more humanoid in appearance, and even gave him that little "nose" from the later Heap stories that to me always resembled a dangling carrot. *Savage Tales* #1 came out dated May 1971, by which time a second Man-Thing story had been scribed by another relative newcomer, Len Wein, and drawn by the amazing Neal Adams. However, Marvel's publisher Martin Goodman got cold feet—or something—and pulled the plug on *Savage Tales* after just one issue, so the second yarn went on the shelf, until it was printed as part of the Ka-Zar (jungle lord) story in *Astonishing Tales* #12 (June 1972). In it, Len had codified a nice embellishment on the protagonist's powers, building on visual clues inherent in but perhaps not consciously intended in Gerry's and my story: namely, if a person felt fear (and who wouldn't, to see such a monstrosity lurching toward him?), his flesh would burn at the Man-Thing's touch.

"Meanwhile"—but surely before he wrote that second Man-Thing story—Len Wein scripted a stand-alone horror/mystery story for DC Comics' anthology title *The House of Secrets* (#92, June-July 1971). "Swamp Thing," moodily drawn by newcomer Berni Wrightson, featured yet another Heap-like entity that ambled out of a marsh to right a wrong; its backstory involved a lab "accident" caused by an envious scientist, who buried his badly wounded colleague alive in "the fetid interior of the swamp beyond"—but there was clearly no particular intent of a sequel.

Comics readers and editor Joe Orlando, however, insisted that this plug-ugly star in a regular series, so Wein and Wrightson's *Swamp Thing* #1 debuted with an Oct.-Nov. 1972 cover date, with an adjusted origin that somewhat resembled Man-Thing's… but then, there are only so many ways you can concoct a muck-monster, right? (At virtually the same time, also with an Oct. '72 date, a full-length Man-Thing series debuted in Marvel's *Fear* #10, again teaming up Gerry Conway and Gray Morrow; he, too, would soon get his own titled mag.)

The swamps were getting crowded. And it wasn't quite over.

Around this same time, Marvel launched a new horror/mystery comic called *Supernatural Thrillers*, for which Stan allowed me to arrange to adapt fiction from prominent fantasy and science-fiction writers. The very first one I went to, phoning him in California from my New York apartment, was Theodore Sturgeon—with whom I immediately arranged for an adaptation of "It." I figured, with Man-Things and Swamp Things and Heaps on the loose, it was high time readers got a chance to get a closer look at the story that had started it all. I wrote that issue myself, of course, utilizing much of Sturgeon's moody prose, and was fortunate to have Marie Severin as

(Main picture below:) The Man-Thing first saw the *(dappled)* light of day in Marvel's black-&-white comic Savage Tales #1 *(May 1971).* The story was plotted by Roy Thomas, scripted by Gerry Conway, and drawn by Gary Morrow - from an original concept by Stan Lee.

(Left top:) The cover of Skywald's black-&-white horror comic Psycho #2 *(May 1971),* the first appearance of that company's Heap, painted by Hector Varella.
(Left middle:) Skywald even published a color The Heap #1 *(Sept. 1971),* with a cover by Tom Sutton & Jack Abel.
(Left bottom:) Over at DC, writer Len Wein and artist Berni Wrightson produced the story "Swamp Thing," intended as a one-off, for The House of Secrets #92 *(June-July 1971).* Cover by Wrightson.

(Main picture below:) Jim Steranko's cover for Supernatural Thrillers #1 (Dec. 1972), wherein writer Roy Thomas and artist Marie Severin adapted Theodore Sturgeon's seminal story "It."

(Right top:) Berni Wrightson's cover for Swamp Thing #1 (Oct. 1972). Script inside by Len Wein.
(Right middle:) Eclipse Comics' Airboy #3 (Aug. 1986) reintroduced Hillman's Heap to the world. Cover pencilled by Stan Woch, with inks by Tim Truman.
(Right bottom:) This panel from the comic book Alter Ego #1 (May 1986) shows young Rob Lindsay being attacked by Uriah Heap and two other rechristened Golden Age bad-guys. Originally published by First Comics. Script by Roy & Dann Thomas, art by Ron Harris.

both penciler and colorist. With inking by Frank Giacoia and behind a cover by Jim Steranko, *Supernatural Thrillers* #1 (Dec. 1972) was a resounding aesthetic success—even if a sequel was more or less precluded. (Stan liked the title "It," though, which he himself had used before for one of his pre-Marvel monster stories, so it was soon given, complete with the logo from *ST* #1, to a series starring an earlier and quite un-Heap-like Lee-Kirby creation.) Though Marvel's adaptation of the Sturgeon story was reprinted in the 1975 black-&-white one-shot *Masters of Terror*, the contracts I'd whipped up with the advice and consent of a Marvel attorney were all eventually lost, so no one today can be clear as to what reprint rights the company might or might not have. Thus, it's unlikely that "It" or most other horror/sf adaptations of that period can ever again be legally reprinted. Pity.

DC's *Swamp Thing* proved to have the greatest "legs" of the Heap wannabes under all that frizz and filth, especially while Wein and Wrightson were teamed on it, and later when writer Alan Moore took it over—but Marvel's Man-Thing likewise had his own title for some time, with Steve Gerber the writer who handled the character in the most Heap-like manner, using him often as a macabre sweeper-up of loose ends, and with Mike Ploog providing some of the most effective art. There were two low-budget but decent *Swamp Thing* movies in the '80s, and one in-name-only *Man-Thing* fiasco of a film for the Sci-Fi Channel in the 2000s. Both characters still make regular reappearances in comic books.

After the '70s, I made one more stab at reviving the Heap myself—more or less. In the four-issue *Alter Ego* comic book series done in 1986 for First Comics of Chicago, artist Ron Harris and I revived Airboy and the Heap as two of the "Limbo Legion," a group that exists in a dimension where the comic book heroes and milieu of the Second World War are real. At the suggestion of editor Mike Gold, Airboy became Flyboy, and the Heap became Uriah Heap, taking his name from a Charles Dickens villain.

Around the same time, Dean Mullaney and his wife cat yronwode, who'd launched a comics company called Eclipse, spoke with me at a San Diego Comic-Con about my writing for their projected revival of the Heap. I accepted, but somehow the agreement fell through the cracks; well, I was busy bouncing between DC and Marvel then, anyway. The original Heap first reappeared in Eclipse's *Airboy* #3 (Aug. 1986), in an exploit written by Chuck Dixon and drawn by Stan Woch & Willie Blyberg. Sky Wolf was back, too.

In fact, *Air Fighters Comics* was back, as well, for Eclipse soon reprinted several of its early-'40s issues with black-&-white interiors, including the Sky Wolf yarn that had introduced the Heap. Finally, in *Air Fighters Classics* #2 (Jan. 1988), more than four decades after I'd first encountered the Heap, I—along with many other readers—got a chance to read his origin story. But it's never been reprinted in *color*—until this volume from PS Artbooks. Bill Black's black-&-white reprint company AC Comics has also reprinted a number of vintage Heap stories over the past two decades or so.

Once Eclipse had folded its tents, there were other attempts to "create" a new and viable Heap. In 1998 Todd McFarlane's hit super-hero comic *Spawn* introduced a Heap who'd been a murdered homeless man… and in 2011 Moonstone Books published a three-issue *Heap* series which owed much to the Hillman feature. Neither of these versions endured, however.

(Below:) A later-years self-portrait of original Sky Wolf/Heap artist Mort Leav seems to be eyeing a sketch of himself and another artist (or maybe it's Harry Stein, lending a helping hand spotting the blacks) at the drawing board in their younger days.

III. The Hillman Heap

And that brings us, full circle, to the original Heap stories of the 1940s and early '50s, which slowly began to be rediscovered from 1988 onward, in the Eclipse and AC reprints.

As we now know, the original Heap was created for a 1942 issue of Hillman Periodicals' *Air Fighters Comics* by the team of writer Harry Stein and artist Mort Leav (not, as some sources assert, by writer William Woolfolk or anyone else).

Hillman Periodicals was founded in 1938 by Alex Hillman, whom Wikipedia lists as "a former New York City book publisher"—and whom 1949-52 Hillman associate editor Herb Rogoff describes (in *Alter Ego* #43, 2004) as "a fat, cigar-smoking tightwad." As per Mike Benton's *The Comic Book in America: An Illustrated History* (Taylor Publishing Co., Dallas, 1989), Hillman was already publishing "movie-star magazines" and the like when it decided in 1940 to dip its toe in comic book waters, starting with the short-lived title *Miracle Comics*, followed by the equally unsuccessful *Rocket Comics* and *Victory Comics*. It was Hillman's fourth entry—*Air Fighters Comics*, debuting for Nov. 1941—that soared highest by far, after, in issue #2, it introduced Airboy, Sky Wolf, and a winning line-up of high-flying heroes.

Sky Wolf, the creation of Harry Stein and Mort Leav, was basically an imitation of Blackhawk, a new hit over in Quality's *Military Comics*. Sporting the aforementioned wolf's-head aviator's helmet, Sky Wolf led a squadron composed of pilots from various countries. The Heap was introduced in the second Sky Wolf outing and faced that hero three more times between 1943 and 1946. The only Heap story Stein and Leav produced was the origin—but of course that's the most important one.

Stein (whose real name has been reported as Harry Smilkestein) had begun his career drawing for Jerry Iger's comics shop in 1939. He has relatively few comic credits in the online Who's Who of American Comic Books 1928-1999 and/or the Grand Comics Database: a few back-up stories for MLJ and Fawcett, a bit of Uncle Sam, Plastic Man, and Blackhawk for "Busy" Arnold's Quality group—and at least the first two Sky Wolf stories for Hillman. After 1942 his only other attributed comics credit is serving as an editor at Quality in 1949.

He and artist Mort Leav (1916-2005), according to a memoir Leav wrote for my comics-history magazine *Alter Ego* in 2002, created the Heap while at Iger. Leav wrote, "We were having a ball coming up with names before settling on 'The Heap'"—though, alas, he didn't name any of the other possibilities. When I asked him if Sturgeon's two-year-old story "It" was an influence, he responded: "I don't know a Theodore Sturgeon." Of course, that doesn't mean that writer Harry Stein hadn't read that horror fantasy, or at least was aware of its plot.

Be that as it may, Stein and Leav's plane-crash-and-swamp origin for the Heap is classic in its own way. The Leav-designed Heap has a very definite pair of eyes, a mouth, even fangs; but eventually his eyes (assuming they still existed) were shrouded behind the swamp-stuff of which he was formed, and the mouth and fangs would likewise disappear for good. The change was, it must be said, a distinct improvement.

Leav, who drew the first four Sky Wolf stories before leaving that aviator in the capable hands of Bob Fujitani, worked in comics till 1954, when he departed for TV advertising. His most celebrated co-creation

is no doubt Mr. Whipple, the imperious supermarket manager who admonished giddy customers not to squeeze the Charmin (toilet paper) in a series of memorable TV ads in the 1960s. We prefer the Heap.

Although the identities of the writers of most of the Heap stories aren't known, those of the artists are often more easily discovered. And the Heap was fortunate to have capable, often exceptional artists—though, being at the dawns of their careers, they were not yet delivering quite the level of work for which they'd later be celebrated. The two dozen tales reprinted in this volume were rendered by a surprisingly small coterie of artists.

Whether or not the second Sky Wolf/Heap encounter was actually drawn by Dan Barry—in the online Grand Comics Database, that credit is followed by a question mark, meaning attribution is uncertain—that artist would definitely illustrate (and sign) several 1947 Heap stories. After doing noted work on Lev Gleason's *Crime Does Not Pay* in the late '40s, Barry would write and/or draw the *Flash Gordon* comic strip for decades.

Paul Reinman, whom I (and perhaps I alone) suspect of being the artist on two or three of the earliest Heap solo sagas, had until recently been drawing Green Lantern exploits for DC—including the first Solomon Grundy story! I feel I detect his work in the Heap stories from *Airboy*, Vol. 3, #10 through V3#12.

Arthur Peddy and Bernard Sachs, a post-WWII team, are best remembered for drawing Justice Society stories in 1948-50 *All-Star Comics*. Sachs would remain in the field long enough to ink its successor, *Justice League of America*, for the first half of the 1960s.

Carmine Infantino would become the artist/co-creator of the Silver Age Flash in 1956, and would eventually become art director and even publisher of DC Comics. He has reported that Hillman editor Ed Cronin encouraged him to *write* some of his Heap stories, though it's impossible to be certain which ones those were. Infantino's art in the last Heap entries seen in this volume show him at the apex of his Milt Caniff-influenced style, before he began to veer toward modernistic design and a more stylized mode of storytelling at DC.

Dick Wood, who's credited as the scripter of at least one Heap story, wrote myriad comics scripts over the years, including DC's Batman and Quality's Blackhawk.

The Grand Comics Database attributes numerous Heap stories in this volume to William Woolfolk, and that later bestselling fiction author did tell Jerry Bails for the Who's Who that he had written some Heap yarns in "1946-47." However, comics script-writing analyst Martin O'Hearn, who's had access to Woolfolk's records of his scripting from Jan. 1945 through Sept. 1947, says Woolfolk "recorded only one story written for Hillman during that period: the Sky Wolf one in *Airboy*, Vol. 2, #11 (Dec. 1945)." Given

Dan Barry — William Woolfolk — Arthur Peddy

Carmine Infantino — Frank Bolle — Leonard Starr

how far in advance of publication dates comic scripts had to be written, that makes it less likely that Woolfolk sneaked in a Heap assignment that is being reprinted in this book…but who knows for certain?

Frank Bolle ably drew, among many other things, a mountain of quality Westerns for Magazine Enterprises from 1948-56 and movie adaptations for Dell in the late '60s.

Leonard Starr, Bolle's early partner and inker, would go on to draw for DC and, beginning in 1957, to have his own popular newspaper strip, *On Stage*.

Of perhaps greater importance than any of the above except creators Stein and Leav was Hillman editor Ed Cronin, who was described by his 1949-52 assistant Herb Rogoff as fair and very talented, if a bit eccentric and absent-minded. Rogoff reported that Cronin often wrote plots for his scripters to flesh out; Jim Amash, who has interviewed Rogoff and several artists about Hillman, says he's come to think of Cronin as essentially the co-writer of many stories he edited, probably including those starring the Heap.

The tales in this volume, by and large, speak for themselves. You'll either like them—and the concept of the Heap—or you won't. Chances are that you'll find the central concept—i.e., the Heap him/itself— more engaging than the individual stories or art. Still, there was thought behind the series, from first to last.

Stein and Leav, right off the bat, conceived of the Heap as a "villain" who had a very human past. True, he was the "undead"/ "unalive" manifestation of an WWI German pilot at a time when the United States was at war with Hitler's resurgent Germany… yet, whether because of a Sturgeon influence or merely out of their own temperaments, they created him as virtually beyond good and evil—a force of nature (or anti-nature), if you will.

Whether 'twas editor Ed Cronin or a writer or artist who came up with the idea, when the Heap was awarded his own series—a borderline brilliant notion all on its own, come to that—the decision was made to humanize the stories by ringing in a teenage boy, Rickie Wood, to be the focus of the stories. The alternative would have been to rely on captions to carry the yarns, which might've been off-putting to readers eager for action and dialogue. Rickie, who would be alternately sympathetic to the Heap and eager to help destroy him (though increasingly the latter), was a forerunner of Rick Jones, the teenager who in 1962 would become the sidekick of Marvel's Hulk, a linear if not imitative descendant of the Heap. Rickie's toy model German plane, which intrigues the Heap because it stirs latent memories of his own past, becomes a bit over-used, perhaps, as the glue that ties boy and behemoth together. Still, it's almost worth it for the playful moment in Vol. 4, #1, when Rickie instead flies a scale model of Airboy's Birdplane!

The Rickie-and-Heap connection was the paramount continuity in the stories until *Airboy Comics*, Vol. 4, #9, when, as Dan Barry began a several-issue stint as the series' artist, a strange and incongruous new element was interjected: a wager made between the Roman deities Ceres and Mars, which I'll let you react to as you read about it. Roping a pair of pagan gods into the mix, and using that first story to write Rickie Wood out of the series, gave a sudden extra air of unreality to the stories, which despite the Heap had been grounded in a relative realism. The added pantheon, however, must have been swiftly considered a failed experiment, for after three issues there was no more mention of the Olympians. I doubt if you'll miss them much.

From that point on, the influence of "crime comics," which reached their apex in the late '40s, is increasingly prevalent in the Heap's adventures. The insertion of horror elements will come in later issues—and will be seen in Volume 2 (forthcoming very soon) of this series.

And now, after this exhaustive (and perhaps exhausting) introduction, it's time to get to the true *raison d'être* of this book: 24 comic book stories featuring the Heap, one of the most unique creations in the history of the medium.

In the parlance of the tales themselves, he may never have quite have truly lived—

But he's certainly never really *died*, either!

Roy Thomas
2012

(Main picture below:) Jack Kirby-pencilled cover for The Incredible Hulk #1 (May 1962).

(Left bottom:) Young Rick Jones tries to lend the Hulk a helping hand in that first issue, in which the monster later affectionately called "Ol' Greenskin" was colored gray. Script by Stan Lee; pencils by Jack Kirby, inks by Paul Reinman.

* None of the solo Heap tales were given individual story titles in the original 1940s comics. For the readers' convenience, these contents pages refer to the stories by the titles assigned to them long after the fact on the Grand Comics Database; those titles are put between brackets.

NOTE:
A question mark after an artist or writer identification means there is more than a reasonable degree of uncertainty as to whether that attribution is accurate.

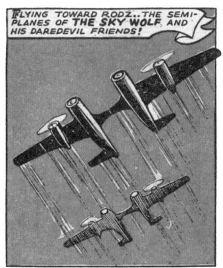

FLYING OVER THE GREAT SWAMP, VON TUNDRA'S PLANES INTERCEPT **THE SKY WOLF'S** CRAFT.. BUT SUDDENLY THE SEMI-PLANES SEPARATE IN MID-AIR...

AND THEIR HALF-PLANE CONSTRUCTION ALLOWS THEM TO NEARLY TOUCH THE NAZIS AND BLAST THEM AT WILL..

THE TURTLE, COCKY AND THE JUDGE CARRY ON A RUNNING DOGFIGHT WITH THE NAZIS..BUT **THE SKY WOLF** AND VON TUNDRA FIGHT ABOVE THE SWAMP..

UNAWARE THAT **SKY WOLF'S** PLANE HAS A FALSE MAIN COCKPIT, VON TUNDRA FIRES IN VAIN.. **SKY WOLF** RIDES IN THE SMALL MOTOR NACELLE!!

WHY ISN'T HE HIT??.. I HAVE DRILLED THAT COCKPIT ENOUGH TO KILL A DOZEN MEN! THE DOG IS CHARMED!

DESPERATELY, VON TUNDRA GAINS ALTITUDE, THEN DIVES STRAIGHT FOR **THE SKY WOLF,**

BUT HE SUCCEEDS ONLY IN STRIKING THE WING OF **THE SKY WOLF'S** SEMI-PLANE..

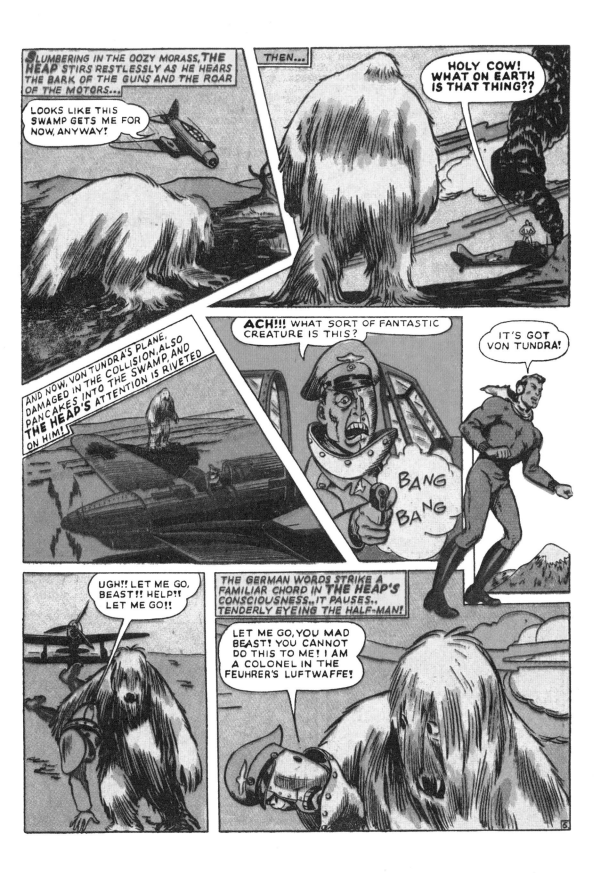

TERRIBLE MOMENTS FOLLOW... HORRIFIED, THE CROWD SEES THE STILL FORM CAST TO THE GROUND..

H'M..DER THINGS DOT **HEAP** DOES GIVES ME AN IDEA! VE COULD USE HIM TO TORTURE POLES! IT VOULD BE NOVEL!

SEIZE DOT THING! WITH HEAVY CHAINS YOU VILL BE ABLE TO TIE HIM UP! QUICK!

UH??

VE GOT HIM!! DER FUEHRER'S SOLDIERS CAN DO ANY'DING!!

COLONEL VON TUNDRA LOOK! VE HAFF DOT NASTY **HEAP** SAFELY TIED UP MIT CHAINS!

AH-H-H.. I FEEL BETTER NOW!

GREETINGS, COLONEL! (BRRRRAAKK) I SEE **THE SKY WOLF** SHOT YOU DOWN AGAIN!! GETTING TO BE A HABIT WITH 'IM, EH?

VE THOUGHT IT VOULDT BE A PLEASANT SURPRISE FOR YOU, COLONEL.. **SKY VOLF'S** PALS.. MAY-BE DEY LIKE TORTURE!

THE SKY WOLF IS PROBABLY DEAD IN THAT SWAMP! HIS MEN ARE OUR PRISONERS! AND WE HAVE AN INGENIOUS NEW METHOD OF TORTURE FOR THESE DUMB POLES! SO..LET US DRINK! HEIL HITLER!

HEIL HITLER!

THE RAT!

BUT SOME DISTANCE BEHIND, SKY WOLF FOLLOWED THE HEAP'S ROUTE TO THE TOWN OF RODZ...AND AFTER NIGHTFALL...

NOW I THINK WE'LL HAVE A LITTLE FUN, MAJOR! TAKE ME BACK TO THOSE FRIENDS OF THE SKY WOLF! I WANT TO WATCH THEIR FACES WHEN I TELL THEM WHAT WE ARE GOING TO DO TO THEM!

♪ OH — VE'LL HANG DER SKY VOLF BY DER TAIL...DUM DE DUM ♪

IT'S FRISCO!! BY GEORGE! — SHE'S PICKING THAT HEINIE MAJOR'S POCKET!!

HA-HA!! THE SKY VOLF'S BRAVE COMRADES DO NOT LOOK SO CHEERFUL — DO THEY, MAJOR?

PSSSST — HERE — THIS MIGHT HELP YOU OUT OF A TERRIBLE TORTURE THEY ARE PLANNING FOR YOU!

COME — LET'S GET BACK TO THE PARTY NOW, GENTLEMEN!

HA! HA! I'D LIKE TO SEE VON TUNDRA'S SO-CALLED FACE WHEN HE LEARNS THAT YOU'RE A.W.O.L. — AND ME ALIVE!!

HOT DARN!! WE'RE ALL SKY WOLVES — AND ONCE AGAIN WE'LL HOWL!!

BUT JUST AS THE FOUR FLIERS ARE ABOUT TO MAKE A QUICK EXIT...

QUICK, LADS, AROUND THIS CORNER!

THE MUTE TURTLE TAPS OUT A MESSAGE ON HIS SKULL... THIS IS HIS "VOICE".

SQUAD, HALT! TAKE DER COFFINS UND LEAVE DEM OUTSIDE! VE USE DEM AFTER DER EXECUTIONS!

LET'S GET INTO THE COFFINS.. THEY'LL CARRY US OUT...

GREAT IDEA, TURTLE!

£PUFF£ £PUFF£ DESE EMPTY COFFINS ARE VERY HEAVY, HERR LIEUTENANT!

BAH! IT ISS JUST DOT YOU ARE GEDDING SOFT SINCE YOU ARE AVAY FROM COMBAT DUTY!

BUT, HERR LIEUTENANT.. DESE COFFINS ARE TOO HEAVY TO BE EMPTY! PERHAPS DERE ISS SOMEDING IN DEM, NEIN?

VOT?

GAAAAA!!! AC-H-H-H-

THEN..

RELAX, RAT! OUR JOB ISN'T GOING TO TAKE VERY LONG!

FORE

UGH!!

28

SKY WOLF

THE HEAP RETURNS !!!
THE SHAPELESS FORM WHICH WAS ONCE THE DASHING BARON EMMELMANN, WORLD WAR GERMAN ACE, MAKES HIS APPEARANCE IN WORLD WAR NO. 2 AS THE "HEAP."... SHOT DOWN OVER A POLISH SWAMP, THE BARON'S INACTIVE BODY MERGED WITH SWAMP VEGETATION — AND ONLY HIS DULLED BUT STRONG MIND LIVED ON! NOW THE HEAP AND SKY WOLF ARE PARTIES TO A STRANGE NEW EPISODE....

WHAT HAS HAPPENED IN THE PAST: TAKEN BY THE NAZIS, THE ODD HEAP WAS CHAINED TO A TREE AND HELPLESS POLISH PRISONERS WERE FORCED TO MARCH WITHIN ITS HUNGRY REACH..... BUT SUDDENLY THE HEAP BREAKS ITS CHAINS, AND FRISCO, GIRL CAFE ENTERTAINER AND FRIEND OF THE SKY WOLF, IS PURSUED BY THE CREATURE!

E-E-K! IT'S AFTER ME!

THE SKY-WOLF IN HIS SEMI-PLANE SEES FRISCO'S DANGER----

I'VE GOT TO GET THAT HEAP AWAY FROM FRISCO- I'LL HAVE TO TAKE A CHANCE WITH A BOMB!

WOW! THAT SHOULD LAND BEHIND THE HEAP-IF MY TIMING WAS RIGHT-OTHER-WISE IT'S TOO BAD FOR HER!

THE LUMBERING HEAP TRIPS AND FALLS, AND THE BOMB STRIKES AHEAD OF HIM....

PLOP!

THE BLAST IS UPWARD AND HE IS UNHARMED.

THE STUNNED CREATURE STAGGERS TO ITS FEET..... AND STUMBLES ALONG AIMLESSLY!

THE SOGGY MIND OF THE EX-GERMAN FLIER BARON VON EMMELMANN STIRS THE HEAP ON----

SOON- AT A NEARBY NAZI AIR FIELD, A PILOT IS READY TO TAKE OFF----

HIMMEL!! IT'S DER HEAP!!

32

LATER... AT A NAZI AIR FIELD... VISITING OFFICIALS VIEW AN AWFUL SCENE....

DONNERWETTER! THE GROUND CREW MURDERED! GASOLINE STORES STOLEN! UND... VOT A MESS!!

LOOK! DISS FELLOW ISS STILL ALIVE!

IT'S.... IT'S A FANTASTIC THING WITH WHITE FUR - IT'S... UGHH......

PERHAPS HE MEANS, SKY WOLF! THAT STUPID FOOL WEARS THE FURRY HEAD OF A WHITE WOLF!

MY AIRDROME HASS BEEN COMPLETELY WIPED OUT! EVERYTHING ISS RUINED! VOT SHALL I DO?

HIMMEL! ANUDDER VUN!

AT THE POLISH UNDERGROUND..

SEND THE MESSAGE-OUR FRIENDS IN ENGLAND MUST HEAR ABOUT THE RUIN AT THE GERMAN AIR BASES!

THE BRITISH INTELLIGENCE GETS THE NEWS....

A LONE CHAP IS RAISING HAVOC WITH THE LUFTWAFFE IN POLAND! IT CAN'T BE ONE OF OUR BOYS!

LET'S CHECK ON SKY WOLF!

SKY WOLF ALSO GETS THE MESSAGE....

SOME FELLOW IS STEALING OUR THUNDER! WONDER WHO HE IS----

WELL, LET'S FIND OUT!

LATER...THE BRITISH INTELLIGENCE CHECKS SKY WOLF AND HIS PALS.....

THE BLOKE ISN'T YOU, AND HE ISN'T ONE OF OURS— WHO IS HE?

I DON'T KNOW. HE'S A POLISH PILOT THE NAZIS HAVEN'T CAUGHT OR HE'S AN ANTI-NAZI GERMAN!

4.

BUT WHOEVER HE IS, WE'RE GOING OVER TO POLAND AND HELP HIM OUT!

GOOD! YOU MEN FIGHTING TOGETHER WILL BE A GREAT HELP TO THE ALLIES!

SOON SKY WOLF AND HIS PALS ARE ROARING TOWARD THE PRIPPET DISTRICT OF POLAND...

WOW! THIS PLACE LOOKS LIKE IT'S BEEN HIT BY A HURRICANE!

SEE ANYBODY DOWN THERE WHO MIGHT TELL US WHAT HAPPENED?

HEY! LOOK!----DOWN THERE- THAT'S AN R.A.F. PILOT- LET'S LAND, MEN_ MAYBE WE CAN DO SOMETHING FOR HIM!

SOME BLOKE.... IN NAZI PLANE.... LANDED, ALL WHITE FUR....ANIMAL FACE.... ATTACKED ME.... TOOK MY PLANE....

GOOD GRAVY!! THAT SOUNDS LIKE THE HEAP!

WELL- THE HEAP'S ALIVE! HE'S FLYING AROUND IN A PLANE, DESTROYING THE NAZIS AND THE ALLIES TOO - WE'VE GOT TO STOP HIM!

IN THE OFFICE OF THE NAZI PROTECTOR OF THE PRIPPET DISTRICT----

DER FUEHRER WARNS ME THAT IF THE CHAOS CAUSED BY THIS ANTI- NAZI IS NOT STOPPED, I VILL BE REMOVED FROM HERE_

POST A REWARD OF 100,000 REICHMARKS FOR THE CAPTURE OF THIS WHITE-FURRED CREA- TURE.. WARN THE PEOPLE THAT FOR EVERY NAZI KILLED, 100 POLES VILL BE EXECUTED!

5.

LATER—A POLISH BOY REPORTS THE NAZI THREAT TO SKY WOLF....

..AND HE WILL KILL 100 OF OUR COUNTRYMEN FOR EVERY NAZI KILLED BY THE WHITE-FURRED BEAST!

THAT'S BAD! ..TURN ON THE RADIO THERE MAY BE MORE NEWS!

=AND AN AERIAL DRAGNET HAS BEEN THROWN AROUND THE PRIPPET AREA! NO ONE WILL ESCAPE OUR VENGEANCE!

HMM! THAT MEANS THE LUFTWAFFE IS COMBING THE PRIPPET MARSHES!

WE MUSTN'T LET THE NAZIS GET THE HEAP! YOU CAN HELP! YOU UNDERGROUND POLISH HAVE A MODEL BRITISH HURRICANE PLANE THAT I CAN USE---- GET IT FOR ME!

YES SIR!

WE'LL KEEP WATCH ON THE LUFTWAFFE RADIO BEAM. ONE OF THEIR PLANES MAY MEET THE HEAP, AND WE'LL KNOW IT AS SOON AS THEY DO!

SOMETIME LATER....THE JUDGE HEARS A FLASH----

ACHTUNG! THERE IT ISS! THE FURRY THING!! AFTER IT MEN!

SKY WOLF! THAT'S IT!! THEY'VE SIGHTED IT!!

LET'S GO, FELLOWS!

WONDER HOW MANY OF THE JERRIES ARE THERE?

MEANWHILE...A SQUADRON OF NAZIS TAKES OFF MILES AWAY----

JA!! WE'RE NEAREST THAT CREATURE! WE SHOULD BE ABLE TO CAPTURE IT AND GET DER FUEHRER'S REWARD!

6

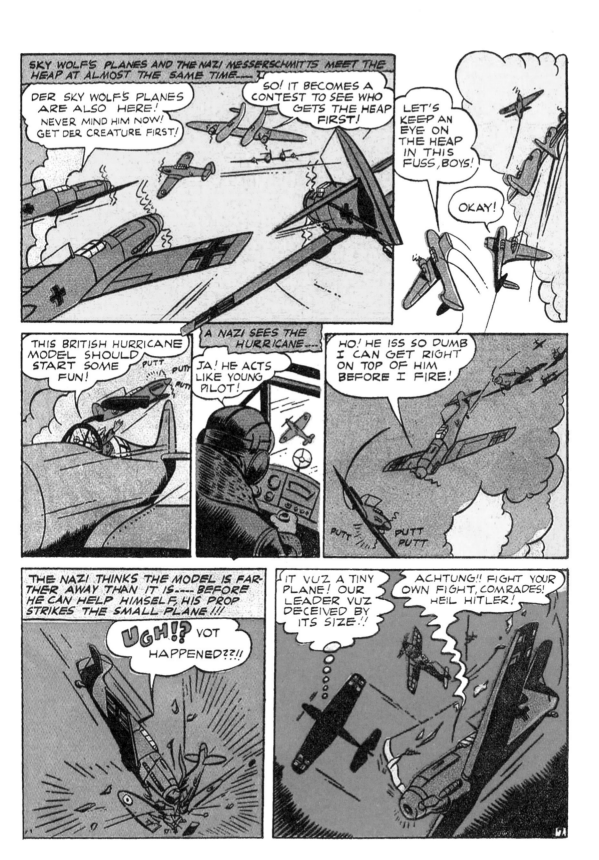

OUR JOB ISN'T DONE YET. WE'RE PAYING HERR NAZI PROTECTOR AN UNINVITED VISIT!

I SEE! WE'LL CLAIM THE REWARD!

THAT'S PARTLY TRUE. WE'LL USE THE MONEY TO HELP POLISH HOSTAGES!

SKY WOLF AND HIS PALS INVADE THE PROTECTOR'S HALLOWED GROUNDS.

GOOD EVENING MY FRIENDS! WE THOUGHT YOU'D ENJOY OUR COMPANY, SO WE CAME!

YOU BET!

ACH! SKY WOLF!

YES! YOU SHOULD KNOW THAT IF YOU TRY TO MURDER INNOCENT PRISONERS YOU'LL HAVE TO DEAL WITH US!

I WOULDN'T PLAY WITH THAT HARDWARE IF I WERE YOU!

OW! YOU WIN!

BANG

WELL— WHAT DO YOU WANT?

YOU POSTED 100,000 REICHMARKS REWARD FOR SHOOTING DOWN THE ANTI-NAZI!! WELL, WE GOT HIM ... THE HEAD!! HERE'S PROOF BY PHOTOGRAPH!

IT WAS ALL A JOKE! I HAVEN'T ANY MONEY!

I SEE! YOU NEVER MEANT TO GIVE A REWARD... BUT YOU'RE GOING TO PAY ANYWAY!

MAKE EVERY BOMB COUNT! WE'RE GOING TO GIVE DER FUEHRER A TASTE OF HIS OWN MEDICINE!

LEAVE IT TO US!

SKY WOLF AND HIS ACES REACH BERCHTESGADEN.

HIMMEL—DER SKY WOLF!! VOT SHALL VE DO?

FUEHRER ORDERED US TO BE VERY QUIET, HE HAS A HEAD-ACHE UND DER GUN VILL DISTURB HIM!

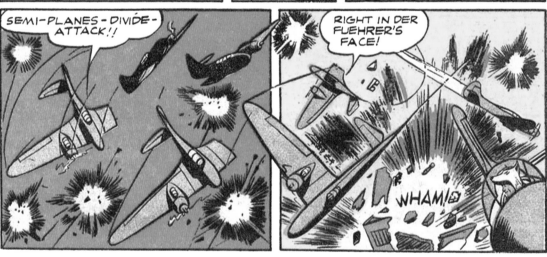

SEMI—PLANES—DIVIDE—ATTACK!!

RIGHT IN DER FUEHRER'S FACE!

WHAM!

VERE ISS OUR LUFTWAFFE! TELL GOERING HE LOSES T'REE MEDALS! BAW!

I T'INK DER FUEHRER ISS ANGRY!

CALLING ALL STAFFELS... SKY WOLF BOMBED BERCHTESGADEN! FORTUNATELY DER FUEHRER IS UNHARMED!!

ACH DU LIEBER! HIMMEL!

I'D BETTER LEAVE THE POLES ALONE NOW! FOR IF SKY WOLF PRINTS THE REQUISITION FORM I SIGNED, DER FUEHRER VILL KILL ME!

AND HERE WE LEAVE SKY WOLF AND HIS PALS... 'TIL THE NEXT ISSUE OF AIR FIGHTERS

THE STRANGE STORY OF BARON VON EMMELMAN BEGINS ON OCTOBER 12, 1918, AT A CERTAIN GERMAN AIRFORCE BASE....

A LETTER FROM YOUR PRETTY WIFE, HERR BARON?

JA! SHE SENT ME A PICTURE OF THE BABY, TOO!

HMMM, VERY CUTE! YOU ARE A LUCKY MAN, HERR BARON!

LUCKY-YES! I CANNOT WAIT FOR THE WAR TO BE FINISHED! NO MAN EVER HAD MORE TO LIVE FOR THAN I HAVE!

THAT SAME DAY BARON VON EMMELMAN LED HIS SQUADRON INTO HIS LAST SKYFIGHT!..

FLAMING LIKE A METEOR, VON EMMELMAN'S PLANE HURTLED FROM THE SKIES... IT WAS THE DEATH PLUNGE!!

LATER, WHEN THE SQUADRON RETURNED TO ITS BASE, A FINAL TOAST WAS DRUNK TO THE BARON --

TO VON EMMELMAN! HE DIED LIKE A TRUE GERMAN!

POOR CHAP! ONLY THIS MORNING HE SAID THAT HE HAD EVERYTHING TO LIVE FOR!

--AND SO THE LIFE STORY OF BARON VON EMMELMAN ENDED--

·········

OR DID IT??

NO ONE COULD SURVIVE THAT CRASH... BUT THE WILL OF BARON VON EMMELMAN TO LIVE WAS SOMETHING THAT DEFIED THE IMPOSSIBLE—

SOMEHOW A TINY FLICKERING SPARK OF LIFE REMAINED. HIS MIND SEEMED DEAD.. HIS BODY MERGED WITH THE VEGETATION, BUT THE DIM BLIND WILL TO LIVE DID NOT CHANGE WITH THE PASSING YEARS--

THE ELEMENTS WORKED ON HIS BATTERED BODY...BUT HE BREATHED AND DREW LIFE FROM THE GROUND LIKE SOME INCREDIBLY PRIMITIVE ANIMAL--AND ONE DAY--

NATURE'S FANTASTIC PRODUCT....BORN OF A DYING MAN'S WILL TO LIVE, WAS REVEALED TO THE WORLD....A FORMLESS MONSTER THAT LEARNED TO FEED ON THE OXYGEN TAKEN FROM THE VEINS OF LIVING CREATURES....

...ITS FIRST VICTIM WAS A HUSKY SHEPHERD DOG... THIS MONSTER SOON WAS KNOWN AS...

.... THE *HEAP!*

THE HEAP BECAME A LEGEND AND A TERROR. PEOPLE, ANIMALS, AND FOWL WERE FOUND HORRIBLY MANGLED...

ALWAYS THE HEAP MOVED ON, ACROSS THE GREAT STEPPES AND FROZEN WASTES OF SIBERIA, IMPELLED BY THE DESPERATE CRAVING FOR FOOD TO MAINTAIN ITS UNNATURAL LIFE---

3

UNTIL FINALLY, SOME-WHERE IN A VILLAGE IN OCCUPIED CHINA!

WE JAPANESE MUSTN'T RUN FROM MONSTER—WE CANNOT SHOW FEAR BEFORE THESE IGNORANT NATIVES!

APPROACH QUIETLY! WE WILL TAKE THE "THING" BY SURPRISE!

THE HEAP IS STUNNED!

CRACK!

ARRGGHH!!

NOTIFY THE MILITARY COMMANDER! TELL HIM WE HAVE CAPTURED A---A "THING" I KNOW NOT HOW TO DESCRIBE!

LATER MOST AMUSING! WE WILL EXHIBIT HIM TO THE WHITE CAPTIVES OF THE MISSION! HE SHALL FEED UPON THE BODY OF THE ENEMY PILOT WHO TRIED TO RESCUE THEM!

MEANWHILE, AT THE HOME BASE OF THE WORLD-FAMED SKY WOLF AND HIS COMPANIONS...

NO WORD FROM TURTLE IN HOURS, "COCKY!"

I'LL BET HE WENT OUT TO RESCUE THOSE MISSION PEOPLE SINGLE-HANDED, SKY WOLF!

HE'D BE BACK NOW--UNLESS SOMETHING WENT WRONG..

WHAT ARE WE WAITING FOR?

RIGHT! WE'LL FIND TURTLE IF IT'S THE LAST THING WE EVER DO!

MOMENTS LATER, SKY WOLF AND "COCKY" TAKE OFF IN SEARCH OF THEIR MISSING COMRADE..

IN THE MEANTIME, THE JAP COMMANDER WATCHES THE HEAP GROW MORE AND MORE FRANTIC FOR FOOD.

HE'S READY NOW! ASSEMBLE THE MISSION CAPTIVES! AND BRING OUT THE ENEMY PILOT!

AS THE MISSION PEOPLE ASSEMBLE...

AH! WELCOME BARONESS VON EMMELMAN! OUR LITTLE SHOW IS ABOUT TO BEGIN!

WHAT MURDEROUS GAME HAS YOUR TWISTED MIND THOUGHT OF THIS TIME?

5

YOU WRONG ME, MY DEAR BARONESS! AFTER ALL, YOUR NATION AND MINE ARE ALLIES!

I LEFT GERMANY MANY YEARS AGO—AFTER MY HUSBAND DIED! NOW MY ONLY CONCERN IS FOR THE SICK AND WOUNDED IN THE LANDS YOUR ARMIES HAVE INVADED!

AH--BUT WE HAVE OUR LITTLE PLEASURES TOO... LOOK!!

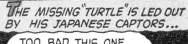

THE MISSING "TURTLE" IS LED OUT BY HIS JAPANESE CAPTORS...

TOO BAD THIS ONE HAS NO TONGUE! OR YOU WOULD HEAR HIM SHRIEK FROM FEAR!

TURTLE IS FORCED INTO THE CAGE WHERE THE HUNGRY AND HALF-CRAZED HEAP AWAITS HIM!

LOCK THE CAGE DOOR! NOTHING CAN SAVE THAT BALDHEAD NOW!

TURTLE STRUGGLES IN VAIN AGAINST THE TREMENDOUS STRENGTH OF THE HEAP. SLOWLY HE IS CRUSHED TOWARDS ITS BLOOD-THIRSTY JAWS...

HORRIFIED, BARONESS VON EMMELMAN SCREAMS

NO! NO!

AS THE HEAP HEARS THE BARONESS VON EMMELMAN SCREAM, HE SUDDENLY RELEASES TURTLE AND TURNS BLINDLY TOWARD THE SOUND.

SHRIEK!

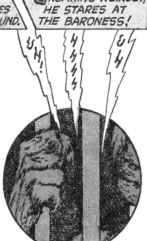

GROANING WEIRDLY, HE STARES AT THE BARONESS!

UH!
UHHH
UH

MOST STRANGE, BARONESS! THE POOR CREATURE SEEMS TO KNOW YOU!

HE'S TRYING TO GET OUT OF THE CAGE!!

UH!

UHHH!

SOMEWHERE IN HIS DIM BRUTE MIND, THE VOICE OF BARONESS VON EMMELMAN AWOKE A RESPONSE; SAVAGELY THE HEAP TEARS AT THE STEEL BARS UNTIL THEY BEND....

ARGHHHH!

BACK! OR I'LL KILL YOU!

THEN---

HELP!
HEL---
AAHAGH

IN A SINGLE LUNGE THE HEAP SWEEPS THE BARONESS INTO HIS MASSIVE ARMS!

HELP!

7

THE MONSTER HAS KILLED OUR COMMANDER! SLAY HIM!

AT THIS MOMENT SKY WOLF AND COCKY, ON THE TRAIL OF THEIR MISSING COMRADE, SEE THE FIGHTING BELOW—

RELEASE THE COUPLINGS! DIVE!

IN A MOMENT THE SEMI-PLANE BECOMES TWO PLANES, AND LIKE TWIN FURIES THEY POUNCE ON THE JAPS!

WE'VE GOT THE JAPS ON THE RUN! NOW'S OUR CHANCE TO FIND OUT WHAT THIS IS ALL ABOUT!

LOOK! THE MISSION PEOPLE AND---!

--AND TURTLE! WE'VE FOUND HIM!

TURTLE'S ALL RIGHT! HELP GET THOSE MISSION PEOPLE INTO OUR PLANES!

WE'D BETTER HURRY! THOSE JAPS WILL BE COMING BACK ANY MINUTE!

THEN SKY WOLF HEARS A FRANTIC CALL....

HELP! PLEASE--

WHAT TH--??

8

CAN THIS CREATURE WHO ONCE WAS A MAN, STILL KNOW GRIEF?.. WHO CAN GUESS WHAT PASSES THROUGH THE HEAP'S MIND AS HE HOLDS THE LIFELESS FORM OF THE WOMAN WHO WAS ONCE HIS WIFE?

... SLOWLY THE HEAP RISES... THERE IS A TERRIBLE PURPOSE NOW IN HIS SHAMBLING WALK....

–A PURPOSE THAT EXPLODES INTO VIOLENT MURDEROUS ACTION!!..

AAA GGGHH AHH

AIEE-E-E-E

BULLETS DO NOT STOP HIM! WE ARE LOST!

BANG!

BANG!

BANG!

BANG!

AT LAST THE TERRIBLE FUSILLADE TAKES EFFECT... THE HEAP STAGGERS, FALLS FORWARD AND LIES STILL...

HE IS DEAD, BUT HE KILLED MANY OF OUR MEN!

IT IS SO... BUT LOOK! THE YANKEE PLANE IS FLYING AWAY!! AIEE!!

INSIDE THE PLANE -- THE MONSTER GAVE US A CHANCE TO SAVE TURTLE AND THE MISSION PEOPLE-- SOMEHOW I ALMOST FEEL SORRY THE HEAP IS DEAD....

BUT IS THE HEAP REALLY DEAD?–OR CAN THE FANTASTIC WILL TO LIVE OF BARON VON EMMELMAN ONCE AGAIN TRIUMPH OVER DEATH ???......

THE RETURN OF THE "HEAP"!!
~~THAT PRANK OF NATURE WHOSE FULL TERROR IS KNOWN ONLY TO THOSE EUROPEANS WHO HAVE BEEN HELPLESS ACTORS WHEN THIS FORMLESS MONSTROSITY EMERGED FROM HIS POLISH SWAMP TO PUSH THE DRAMA OF WAR INTO THE BACKGROUND~~AND THIS THING WHICH WAS BORN OF A BRAVE FLIER'S WILL TO LIVE MIGHT HAVE BEEN KEPT OUT OF AMERICA~~ BUT FOR ONE MAN'S VANITY!

THE HOME OF PROFESSOR HERMAN KRINGLE, NOTED ZOOLOGIST, ON THE OUTSKIRTS OF A SMALL EAST COAST TOWN—

WELL, IT'S ABOUT TIME YOU CAME WITH THE MAIL!

SORRY, MRS. KRINGLE, BUT YOU'RE QUITE A WAY OUT, YOU KNOW!

ANOTHER LETTER WITH A FOREIGN STAMP FOR YOU, SHRIMP! FROM ONE OF YOUR STUPID EUROPEAN FRIENDS I SUPPOSE!

THANK YOU, MY DEAR!

MY DEAR PROFESSOR; "THE HEAD" WILL ARRIVE ON THE FREIGHTER "LAMSON" ON THE DATE YOU WISHED. WHY YOU WANT THIS DEAD HULK OF THE FAMOUS FLIER, BARON VON EMMELMAN IS STRANGE INDEED. YOUR $25,000. PAYMENT WAS RECEIVED! CRE...

WELL, WHAT IS IT NOW? LET ME SEE THAT LETTER!

NO, NO, ELIZABETH! THIS IS ONE LETTER I CANNOT SHOW YOU!

GIVE ME THAT LETTER, YOU LITTLE HOUND.... OHHH....

SORRY MY LOVE! THE FIRE'S GOT IT NOW!

A FEW NIGHTS LATER, PROFESSOR KRINGLE KEEPS A MIDNIGHT APPOINTMENT AT THE WHARF—

OKAY, PROFESSOR. I WAS PROMISED FIVE GRAND TO SMUGGLE THIS CRATE INTO THE COUNTRY!

HERE IT IS, MY MAN—AND "SILENCE" IS THE WORD...

LATER AT THE PROFESSOR'S HOME ——

WHEW! SOME LOAD! WHAT HAVE YOU GOT HERE, PROFESSOR?

EQUIPMENT—JUST EQUIPMENT! PUT IT IN THAT BUILDING! THANK YOU!

THE PROFESSOR UNPACKS THE CRATE, AND----

AH, MY POWERFUL "HEAP"--YOU HAVE BEEN DEAD MANY MONTHS---BUT YOU CAME BACK TO LIFE BEFORE AND THIS SERUM WILL DO IT FOR YOU AGAIN!

HERMAN! WHAT HAVE YOU GOT IN THERE? SPEAK UP! WHAT ARE YOU DOING?

GO TO BED, ELIZABETH!

BED NOTHING! I'LL SEE FOR MYSELF!

YES, ELIZABETH-- THAT'S A GOOD IDEA, DO SEE FOR YOURSELF!

--AND THE PROFESSOR WATCHES AS THE HORRIBLE SHAPE OF THE "HEAP" ADVANCES TOWARD HIS WIFE---

Yllllll!

YOU WRETCHED WOMAN! MY VENGEANCE HAS FINALLY COME!

THE "HEAP" HAS DONE WHAT I LACKED THE COURAGE TO DO--KILL MY WIFE! BUT NOW, WITH HIM BESIDE ME, I NEED NOT BE A WEAKLING ANY LONGER!

HELP!

!!AGGHHHH

OHHHH

WELL DONE "HEAP"! YOU ARE MY SLAVE, DO YOU HEAR? I HAVE GIVEN YOU LIFE, AND YOU WILL BE MY STRENGTH AND COURAGE IN RETURN---!

3

THE "HEAP" TOSSES THE PORT INSPECTORS ABOUT LIKE TOYS --

HURRY, "HEAP"! HURRY! WE MUST ESCAPE!

AH, "HEAP", YOU HAVE DONE FINE INDEED! WE ARE GOING TO BE GREAT FRIENDS, I THINK!

LATER SKYWOLF READS THE NEWS TO HIS PAL, "COCKY" ROACH!

"MAD PROFESSOR AND MONSTER RUN AMUCK" -- COCKY, THERE'S NO DOUBT ABOUT IT THIS CREATURE THEY'RE TALKING ABOUT IS THE "HEAP" ALL RIGHT!

IT SAYS IN THE PAPER THAT THE POLICE ARE LOOKING FOR THE "HEAP" AND KRINGLE!

NOW WHERE COULD THE "HEAP" AND KRINGLE HIDE OUT NOW!

KRINGLE'S HOME WAS ONLY FOUR MILES FROM THE NAVY SEA PLANE BASE HERE! IF THE "HEAP" IS VON EMMELMAN THE FLIER, I'LL BET HE'D HEAD HERE!

COULD BE, SKYWOLF! LET'S GIVE IT A TRY---

MINUTES LATER SKYWOLF AND COCKY. IN THEIR SEMI-PLANE APPROACH THE NAVY AIR BASE ---

WELL- HERE WE GO DOWN, COCKY!

AS THE HUGE CRAFT TAKES TO THE AIR, COCKY WINGS ALONGSIDE--

WHAT A MESS! I CAN'T SHOOT THE "HEAP" AND KRINGLE DOWN BECAUSE SKYWOLF IS IN WITH THEM!

WHILE IN THE "MARS"--

OH-OH!! THAT BIG "FLEA-BAG" IS BUSTING OUT THROUGH THE PLANE'S TOP!

CRASH!!

HEAVEN KNOWS I'VE GOT A BIG ENOUGH PROBLEM MYSELF-- SAY--A CHUTE!

WHAT A BREAK-- NOW MAYBE I CAN SET FIRE TO THIS FLYING FERRY-BOAT AND SAVE MY NECK--

SKYWOLF SETS FIRE TO THE PLANE----

--- RIGHT UNDER THE WING GAS TANK---THAT SHOULD TAKE CARE OF THIS SITUATION!

BOY! LOOK AT THAT FIRE!--WELL, I GUESS I'LL BOW OUT NOW!

9

AT A GERMAN AIRFIELD DURING WORLD WAR I.

I CAN'T BELIEVE IT! OUR GREAT VON EMMELMAN..*DEAD!*

YES..I SAW HIM GO DOWN..IN THE GREAT POLISH SWAMP..

VON EMMELMAN WAS SO GALLANT! HE OFTEN *SWORE* HE WOULD *LIVE* TO SEE US VICTORIOUS!

AND NOW HE LIES OUT IN THE LONELY SWAMPS LIKE SOME FORGOTTEN *THING!*

YES...IT LOOKS LIKE THE END OF THE TRAIL FOR VON EMMELMAN!

BUT WHAT'S THIS!!..IT IS SEVERAL YEARS LATER AND A SHAGGY HULK THAT MOVES LIKE A *MAN* WANDERS ABOUT IN THE DESOLATE DEPTHS OF THE POLISH SWAMP!..IT IS A *CREATURE* WHOSE BODY HAS BEEN MERGED WITH THE VEGETATION...

THE HEAP'S ONLY FOOD OF LIFE IS *OXYGEN!*..OXYGEN THAT WILL BE TAKEN FROM THE BODIES OF OTHER CREATURES WHEN NECESSARY...FOR EVEN LIKE A GREAT EVIL *PLANT*, THE *HEAP* MUST *LIVE!*

AND SO...FOR THIS MONSTER, THE YEARS MOVE ON...

1919 1928 192 1930 1945 1946 1923 1937

2

AND IN 1946, A MADMAN HAD THE *HEAP* SHIPPED TO AMERICA...

5¢ .... WORLD TELEGRAPH ...... 5¢

HEAP BELIEVED DESTROYED IN CRASH OF FLYING BOAT!

MONSTER OF THE AGE PROBABLY PERISHES AT SEA

THE HEAP

IN THE SMALL TOWN OF *LAWNDALE*..RICKIE WOOD TALKS WITH HIS FATHER...

THAT'S QUITE A MODEL YOU HAVE THERE, RICKIE! BUT WHY THE *NAZI* MARKINGS?

OH, IT'S SUPPOSED TO BE A *REAL* MODEL OF A NAZI PLANE, DAD. COME ON OUT..I'M GOING TO FLY IT.

THERE SHE GOES! LOOK AT HER CLIMB!

SOMETHING'S *WRONG!* SHE DIDN'T CIRCLE.. SHE'S FLYING STRAIGHT AHEAD!

BUT AS THE LITTLE NAZI PLANE ZOOMS TO EARTH IN THE WOODS, IT IS WATCHED ...BY THE *HEAP!*

SHE WENT DOWN IN THE WOODS..I'LL HAVE TO GO AND GET HER!

I'LL SEE YOU AT THE HOUSE, RICKIE!

THE MIGHTY *HEAP* CATCHES THE MODEL PLANE...

THE GERMAN MARKINGS ON THE MODEL BRING EXCITEMENT TO A SLUGGISH BRAIN THAT STRUGGLES TO REMEMBER!

AND NOW IT ALL COMES BACK..THE *HEAP* SEEMS TO ONCE AGAIN CONNECT HIMSELF WITH A HANDSOME GERMAN FLIER..AND FIGHTING PLANES IN THE AIR...AND HE HUGS THE "MODEL OF MEMORIES"..

WHILE RICKIE WOOD APPROACHES THE SCENE...

IT WENT DOWN SOMEWHERE IN HERE.

OHH.. GOSH!

WHAT *IS* THAT THING!..AND IT HAS MY *MODEL*!

RICKIE IS AGAIN SET DOWN..AND AS HE WALKS OFF THE *HEAP* SHAMBLES ALONG BESIDE HIM..

GOSH..THIS AWFUL THING SEEMS TO *LIKE* ME! MAYBE IT'S *HUNGRY!*

SUDDENLY, THE *HEAP* COLLAPSES TO THE GROUND..IT IS HUNGRY- BUT NOT FOR THE *KIND* OF FOOD THAT RICKIE THINKS!

EVEN A *MONSTER* LIKE *THAT* HAS TO *EAT!* I'LL SEE WHAT I CAN GET!

IT'S SO *BIG* THAT IT PROBABLY EATS LIKE AN *ELEPHANT!*

A SCREAM FROM OUTSIDE INTERRUPTS RICKIE!

EEE-EEK! EEEKKK!

AS RICKIE RUNS OUTSIDE...

HELP! HELP! CALL THE POLICE!

WHAT'S THE MATTER?

IT'S AWFUL...A GREAT HAIRY MONSTER HAS SNATCHED MY DOG!...IT CAME OUT OF THE WOODS!

WHAT?!

I'LL SEE IF I CAN STOP HIM!

CLUTCHING THE SQUEALING DOG, THE HEAP HESITATES AS IT SEES RICKIE..

THE DOG IS RELEASED AND RUNS OFF... STUPIDLY THE HEAP LOOKS AT RICKIE WHO POINTS TO THE BASKET OF MAN'S FOOD...

...THE MONSTER CONSIDERS A LARGE PIECE OF MEAT FOR A MOMENT, BECAUSE THIS COMES CLOSEST TO HIS NATURAL FOOD!

GOSH..HE DOESN'T SEEM TO BE EATING THE MEAT ..HE'S SQUEEZING IT !!

7

BUT LITTLE DOES RICKIE REALIZE THE TERRIBLE MANNER IN WHICH THE *HEAP* "EATS"...AND HE IS *SAFE* WITH THE MONSTER ONLY BECAUSE OF THE GERMAN PLANE MODEL...*

*...WHICH THE *HEAP* ASSOCIATES WITH THE BOY...

THE POLICE ARE COMING! WHAT A *SURPRISE* THEY'LL *GET* WHEN THEY SEE THIS MONSTER *NIGHTMARE!*

HEY! WHERE ARE YOU GOING? ...YOU DON'T LIKE THE *POLICE*, EH?

THE *HEAP* AGAIN LUMBERS INTO THE WOODS AT THE SOUND OF THE POLICE SIREN...

OKAY..BUT I'LL HAVE TO SEND THEM AFTER YOU!

...AND THIS MONSTER IS ABOUT *SEVEN* FEET TALL..AND IT'S COVERED WITH *GRASS* AND *ROOTS!* IT ISN'T AN ANIMAL, AND IT ISN'T A *MAN*..

WHAT KIND OF A *RIDDLE* IS THIS, KID? *GRASS..ROOTS*..NOT AN *ANIMAL*, AND NOT A *MAN!* COME ON, KELLY...LET'S GET BACK BEFORE WE'RE NUTS!

..AND LISTEN, BOY..YOU OUGHTA *WRITE* ADVENTURE STORIES FOR THE *RADIO* OR SOMETHING..THERE'S *MONEY* IN THAT KIND OF *STUFF!*

I DON'T *BLAME* THEM FOR NOT BE-LIEVING IT!

AND THE UNSUSPECTING RICKIE GOES BACK TO THE *HEAP*...WHO NEVER HAS BEEN SO *CLOSE* TO A *HUMAN* THAT HE DIDN'T *KILL*... BUT NOW HE LOOKS AT THE BOY STUPIDLY AND THINKS OF THAT *GERMAN* PLANE!

WHAT I'D LIKE TO KNOW IS...WHERE YOU CAME FROM... AND *WHAT* YOU ARE...

THE HEAP

It WAS LONG AGO, DURING THE FIRST WORLD WAR THAT GERMANY'S FLYING ACE, BARON VON EMMELMAN, CRASHED IN FLAMES IN A POLISH SWAMP... BUT HIS FIERCE WILL TO LIVE KEPT A SPARK OF LIFE FLICKERING IN HIS BATTERED BODY... A SPARK THAT RESULTED IN A CREATURE THAT WAS TO BE NEITHER ANIMAL NOR MAN... BUT A THING THAT EUROPEANS CAME TO KNOW AS THE HEAP!!... AND A MADMAN BROUGHT IT TO AMERICA... AND IN THE WOODS NEAR LAWNDALE, U.S.A., THE HEAP SAW A SMALL NAZI PLANE MODEL THAT WAS OWNED BY THE BOY, RICKIE WOOD... AND THUS BEGAN THE CREATURE'S STRANGE ATTRACTION TO RICKIE....

THERE YOU ARE, RICKIE ...A FULL BASKET! SAY, WHAT DO YOU *DO* WITH ALL THE MEAT AND VEGETABLES THAT YOU BUY FROM ME?

OH...IT'S FOR A CAMPING CLUB THAT I BELONG TO, MR. ROGERS.

HMM...THAT'S A *LOT* OF FOOD... EVEN FOR A CAMPING CLUB!

I'LL JUST LEAVE THE BASKET HERE. THAT BIG THING IS AROUND SOME-WHERE AND HE'LL FIND IT. I WONDER WHAT KIND OF A CREATURE HE REALLY IS..AND WHERE HE CAME FROM...

BUT RICKIE WOOD'S WORDS STICK IN HIS THROAT...FOR THERE THE HEAP IS!

THE MONSTER THROWS TWO GIGANTIC FORM-LESS PAWS OVER THE BOY IN A SHOW OF AFFECTION........ .. RICKIE IS SPEECH-LESS WITH FEAR..

..BUT HE DOESN'T RUN...BECAUSE THIS HAS HAPPENED BEFORE..

BUT AS THE BOY STARTS TO WALK AWAY, THE *HEAP* FOLLOWS HIM...

RICKIE WOOD HAS COME TO THE EDGE OF THE WOODS...AND NOW HE LOOKS DOWN INTO THE VALLEY...

BOY! WHAT A SWELL VIEW OF THE CARNIVAL FROM UP HERE!

AT THE SIGHT OF THE TENTS, THE HEAP RETREATS TO A LOG...AND TRIES HARD TO RECALL FORMER TENTS...AND A LITTLE BOY AT A CARNIVAL IN GERMANY ...A LONG TIME AGO...

I WONDER WHAT'S THE MATTER WITH HIM...

WHILE DOWN AT THE CARNIVAL...CHUCK THE FLIER TRIES TO 'DRUM UP' BUSINESS...

TAKE A PLANE RIDE, FOLKS..ONLY TWO BUCKS!

FLY for $2.00
15 MINUTES of THRILLING EXCITEMENT with CHUCK PARKIN EX-FIGHTER PILOT

NO! I WON'T CUT THE PRICE TO A DOLLAR! TWO BUCKS OR NOTHING!

OKAY..BUT IT'S A LOT OF MONEY!

AND SOON..AS CHUCK'S PLANE ROARS THROUGH THE AIR, IT IS WATCHED BY THE HEAP!

THE SIGHT OF THE PLANE STIRS OLD MEMORIES WITHIN THE SLOW, SLUGGISH MIND OF THE CREATURE..

4

AND BECAUSE HE DOESN'T SEE THE FAMILIAR GERMAN MARKINGS ON THE CRAFT, THE HEAP BEGINS TO TEAR IT TO SHREDS AS IF IT WERE A RAG DOLL!

CARTER! CARTER! COME QUICK! THERE'S SOMETHING LIKE A BIG APE LOOSE OUT HERE! IT'S RUINED CHUCK'S PLANE ALREADY!

HUH?

HOLY SMOKE! WHAT IS IT? I NEVER SAW ANYTHING LIKE IT!!

ME NEITHER!

WE GOTTA GET EVERY MAN.. HEY RUBE! HEY RUBE! GET THE ELEPHANT GUN! HEY RUBE!

RICKIE WOOD HAS AGAIN LOCATED THE HEAP AND HE COMES RUNNING...

GOSH..HE'S WRECKED THAT PLANE!

THEY'RE TRYING TO CATCH HIM WITH NETS!..HE SEES ME!

WE DON'T LIKE OUTSIDERS TO HIT CARNIVAL PEOPLE, **CHUM!** GOOD-BYE!

HERE HE IS, FOLKS..HERE HE IS!..THE **MARTINIQUE MAN-EATER!**..AND HE IS ONLY **ONE!** SEE THE OTHERS ON THE **INSIDE** FOR **ONE DIME!!**

AND SOON..ROPES HAVE BEEN THROWN ABOUT THE LIFELESS HEAP..AND WITH MUCH STRUGGLING HE HAS BEEN PLACED ON A SIDE-SHOW PLATFORM..

BUT RICKIE WOOD HAS HIS OWN IDEAS ABOUT THE HEAP!

THE **FOOLS!** IF I DON'T CUT THAT MONSTER **LOOSE,** THEY'LL FIND **ALL** THESE BOOBS **DEAD** IN THE MORNING!

RICKIE MAKES A DASH TO CUT THE HEAP'S ROPES..THE MONSTER RECOGNIZES HIM AND SEEMS TO COME TO LIFE AGAIN!..

BEFORE THE BOY CAN EVEN **TOUCH** THE ROPES, THE **HEAP** SNAPS THEM LIKE **TWINE!**

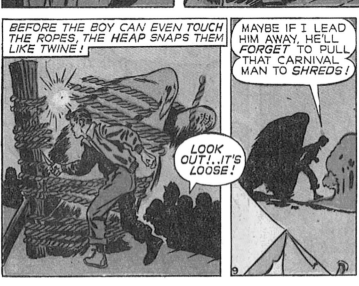

LOOK OUT!..IT'S LOOSE!

MAYBE IF I LEAD HIM AWAY, HE'LL **FORGET** TO PULL THAT CARNIVAL MAN TO **SHREDS!**

I CAN FEEL HIS EYES BURNING RIGHT THROUGH ME! GOSH...AND HOW CAN **I TELL** WHAT THIS CREATURE MIGHT **DO,** ANYMORE THAN ANYONE ELSE..I DON'T EVEN KNOW **WHY** HE **LIKES** ME!

...BUT WE DO, RICKIE! IT'S BECAUSE HE SAW YOU WITH THAT MODEL GERMAN PLANE!

IT WAS DURING WORLD WAR #1 THAT OUR STORY HERE REALLY BEGAN... FOR IT WAS THEN THAT THE BOLD GERMAN FLIER, BARON VON EMMELMAN WAS SHOT DOWN OVER A LONELY POLISH SWAMP, TO BE GIVEN UP FOR DEAD... BUT NATURE PLAYED A GHASTLY TRICK... AND FROM A SPARK OF LIFE, PLUS VEGETATION, THE STRANGE PLANT-LIKE *HEAP* BEGAN!

THE HEAP

....BUT THE MONSTER TURNS AWAY WITHOUT MAKING ANY ATTEMPT TO HURT RICKIE...

I WONDER WHY HE ALWAYS WANTS THIS GERMAN MODEL? ...WELL ANYWAY, I'LL GET RID OF THAT HEAP NOW!

...HE WON'T SEE ANY MORE OF ME OR THE MODEL, ONCE I GET ON THE EXPRESS!

BUT AS RICKIE'S TRAIN PULLS OUT, THE HEAP'S FIERCE EYES WATCH IT FROM THE WOODS...

THE MONSTER REALIZES THAT THE TRAIN IS CARRYING THE THING THAT IS HIS LAST LINK WITH THE PAST...A PAST THAT ONCE SAW HIM AS THE BOLD GERMAN FLIER, BARON VON EMMELMAN OF WORLD WAR I...BEFORE NATURE MERGED HIS DYING BODY WITH THE GROWTH OF A POLISH SWAMP!

STUPIDLY, THE HEAP LUNGES AT THE STARTING LOCOMOTIVE AS THOUGH TO OVERCOME IT..BUT EVEN WITH HIS GREAT WEIGHT, IS BOUNCED BACK INTO THE AIR!

FOR A MOMENT THE HEAP IS DAZED BY HIS DEFEAT...THEN HIS EYES BURN FIERCELY AS HE SEES A MAN OPERATING A HANDCAR COMING DOWN THE TRACK...

MEANWHILE ON THE TRAIN...

HEADED FOR NEW YORK, EH, SON?

YES SIR! AND I CAN'T WAIT TO GET THERE!

BUT RICKIE'S TRIP WOULD BE LESS HAPPY IF HE KNEW THAT THE HEAP HAD KNOCKED THE HANDCAR OPERATOR SENSELESS...AND WAS NOW SPEEDING AFTER THE TRAIN!

AT NATIONAL MODEL HEADQUARTERS IN NEW YORK...

THAT'S QUITE A LITTLE MODEL YOU HAVE THERE, RICKIE!

SHE'S A DANDY!.. WHEN DOES THE MEET BEGIN?

RIGHT NOW, RICKIE! OKAY, FELLOWS, LINE UP FOR THE HIGH-SPEED CONTEST! RICKIE WOOD WILL FLY FIRST!

OKAY BABY! ..SHOW 'EM HOW GOOD YOU ARE!

ONCE-TWICE-RICKIE'S PLANE CIRCLES THE HALL.. THEN AS THE AUDIENCE ROARS ITS APPROVAL, THERE IS AN INTERRUPTION...

BEFORE THE STARTLED AUDIENCE CAN MOVE, THE ELEVATOR DOORS BURST OPEN AND OUT COMES *THE HEAP!*

GET OUT OF HERE QUICK! THERE'S A *MONSTER* IN THE ELEVATOR SHAFT!

THE HEAP!

HE SEES ME! HE'S AFTER MY PLANE AGAIN!

MAYBE I CAN LEAD HIM OUTSIDE ..AWAY FROM THESE PEOPLE!

TO ROOF

IF HE GETS LOOSE IN A CROWD, HE'LL MAIM DOZENS OF FOLKS. COME ON, YOU MONSTER, YOU WANTED TO CATCH ME!

I DON'T KNOW HOW LONG I CAN KEEP THIS UP!

HERE COME THE POLICE... IF I CAN ONLY HOLD OUT!

DRUGS

THE POLICE SOON ARE ON THE ADJOINING ROOF...

THERE IT IS! DO SOMETHING QUICK!

SUFFERING CATS! WHAT IS IT?

DUCK, SONNY! WE'RE GOING TO START FIRING!

THE HEAP DOES NOT PAUSE AS THE BULLETS GO THROUGH HIS HULKING FORM..

BULLETS DON'T HURT THAT THING ..THEY GO RIGHT THROUGH IT!

SWING THIS LADDER OVER ON THE OTHER ROOF! WE'LL ALL RUSH HIM!

THE POLICE LADDER SWINGS TO THE NEXT BUILDING AND THE HEAP WAITS UNTIL THE POLICE ARE HALFWAY ACROSS..THEN..

GO BACK! GO BACK! HE'S GOING TO KNOCK THE LADDER OVER!

STRAIGHT AT THE HEAP'S FACE SPEEDS THE MODEL PLANE.

AND BEFORE HE CAN DODGE IT, THE PLANE HITS HIM AND HE TOPPLES OVER INTO SPACE...

GOOD LAD.. I THOUGHT *WE WERE DONE* FOR!

I JUST HOPE THAT *THING* IS!

HE MUST HAVE LANDED IN THAT GARDEN!...HE'S PROBABLY SQUASHED TO A PULP!

BUT WHEN THEY REACH THE GROUND..

MY GOSH! *LOOK!*

HE'S GROWING *ROOTS* WHERE HE LANDED!...JUST LIKE A *BIG PLANT!*

GET AN AXE QUICK! WE'LL HAVE TO FINISH HIM OFF FAST!

LET ME TAKE ONE OF THESE...THE HEAP IS GROWING FASTER EVERY MINUTE!

IT'S FANTASTIC!

DESPERATELY, THE AXES ARE SWUNG AGAINST THE HEAP'S BODY...BUT EACH WOUND HEALS INSTANTLY...

IT DOESN'T DAMAGE HIM.. IT'S LIKE CHOPPING JELLY!

SUDDENLY LIKE SOME GREAT BUSH, THE HEAP TEARS HIMSELF FROM THE GROUND.

HE'S LOOSE! LOOK OUT!

HE'S GONE! I WANT EVERY MAN IN THE CITY CALLED OUT! WE'VE GOT TO GET THAT THING!

AND LATER...AFTER HOURS OF SEARCHING WITHOUT RESULTS, RICKIE IS AGAIN HEADED FOR HOME...

SO THE POLICE COULDN'T FIND HIM...WELL, I HOPE THAT MEANS HE'S GONE SO FAR HE WON'T BOTHER ME ANYMORE...

THAT'S WHAT YOU THINK, RICKIE!

RICKIE WOOD HAS MADE THE TRIP FROM HIS HOME IN LAWNDALE TO NEW YORK POLICE HEADQUARTERS.

I CAME JUST AS SOON AS I GOT YOUR WIRE, CHIEF KENDEL!

GOOD BOY, RICKIE! YOU'RE THE ONLY ONE WHO KNOWS ANYTHING ABOUT THIS MONSTER OR WHERE HE MIGHT BE HIDING IN THE CITY!

THERE WOULD BE A PANIC IF IT WERE KNOWN THAT SUCH A CREATURE IS LOOSE IN THE CITY!

FOR SOME REASON HE IS ATTRACTED TO THIS MODEL GERMAN PLANE, PERHAPS IF I DROVE AROUND THE CITY WITH IT, HE MIGHT MAKE HIM- SELF KNOWN!

FINE! I'VE GOT A SQUAD CAR AND OFFICER FOR YOU.. GOOD LUCK!

THANK YOU, SIR!

SAY, HOW CAN A BIG THING LIKE THAT HIDE IN THIS CITY?

HE'S NEITHER HUMAN NOR ANIMAL, OFFICER! HE GROWS LIKE A PLANT AND CAN MAKE HIMSELF LOOK LIKE A TREE OR BUSH! HE'S AWFUL!

MEANWHILE, AT CENTER MUSIC HALL, A NEW PICTURE HAS JUST ENDED...

WOW! WHAT A TERRIBLE MOVIE THAT WAS!

I'LL NEVER GO TO SEE A VON MUNCHEN PRODUCTION AGAIN!

LOVE DUST
A VON MUNCHEN PRODUCTION

AND AT ANOTHER EXIT, VON MUNCHEN HIMSELF LEAVES...

VON MUNCHEN, THIS IS YOUR FIFTH FLOP PICTURE! YOU'D BETTER GIVE UP THE MOVIE BUSINESS!

NEVER! I VILL YET MAKE THE GREATEST FILM EVER SEEN! COME AND DINE WITH ME AND I VILL TELL YOU ABOUT IT!

2

LISTEN TO ME, YOU FOOLS! SOME TERRIBLE KIND OF CREATURE IS OVER THERE!

WHY DON'T YOU STOP PULLING THESE GAGS, MUNCHEN?

OH WELL, LET'S LOOK!

AS THE MEN APPROACH HIM, THE HEAP ONCE MORE MERGES WITH THE VEGETATION AND MAKES HIMSELF PART OF THE BUSH...

OKAY, VON MUNCHEN! WHERE IS THIS CREATURE?

IT VOS RIGHT HERE!

WE'VE PLAYED ALONG WITH YOUR GAG, NOW YOU'D BETTER SEE A GOOD DOCTOR!

YEAH! MAKING THOSE CORNY MOVIES HAS DRIVEN YOU NUTS!

GO ON HOME, AND YOU'LL FEEL BETTER, VON MUNCHEN!

NO! NO! I'M GOING BACK TO THE MUSIC HALL! GOOD NIGHT!

AS VON MUNCHEN HEADS FOR THE STAGE DOOR OF THE MUSIC HALL, THE HEAP FOLLOWS HIM...

I CANNOT UNDERSTAND IT! I KNOW I SAW SOMETHING! IT WAS MOVING TOO!

STAGE DOOR

GOOD EVENING, JOSEPH! I THOUGHT I WOULD STOP BY FOR A WHILE!

SURE, MR. VON MUNCHEN! THERE'S NOBODY HERE BUT THAT LADY HIGH-WIRE ARTIST WHO'S REHEARSING ON THE STAGE!

HE'S A NICE FELLOW..TOO BAD HIS PICTURES ARE SO TERRIBLE!

ACT #2

AS JOSEPH TURNS, A DOOR CRASHES OPEN AND THE HEAP COMES TOWARD HIM...

EE..YOW!

MEANWHILE ON A NEARBY STREET, RICKIE WOOD CONTINUES HIS SEARCH...

I'VE GOT TO FIND THAT *THING!*

TAXI!

UG STORE

RICKIE OVERHEARS VON MUNCHEN'S FRIENDS TALKING...

IMAGINE! VON MUNCHEN SAYING HE SAW A *MONSTER!*

I GUESS THIS LAST FLOP JUST ABOUT FINISHED HIM OFF!

EXCUSE ME, BUT DID YOU SAY SOMETHING ABOUT A *MONSTER?*

HA-HA..IT'S NOTHING, SON! A PAL OF OURS SEES TOO MANY *MOVIES!*

HE WAS TRYING TO MAKE A "KING KONG" OUT OF AN OVERGROWN BUSH..BUT DON'T WORRY...HE'S SAFE IN THE MUSIC HALL NOW!

MUSIC HALL?

I'M GOING IN THE MUSIC HALL FOR A MINUTE, OFFICER!

5

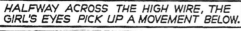

DESPERATELY, RICKIE SWINGS A STAGE BRACE AT THE HEAP...

LET GO! LET GO!

VON MUNCHEN BREAKS LOOSE AND CLIMBS THE LADDER TO THE HIGH WIRE.

SAVE YOURSELF, BOY! I CAN WALK THE WIRE! I'LL BE SAFE!

I HOPE I CAN WALK THE WIRE AS I DID YEARS AGO!

AS VON MUNCHEN STARTS ACROSS THE WIRE HE SEES THE GIRL—AND...

CORA!

CARL!

CORA! GO BACK! GET OFF THE WIRE!

I-I CAN'T ..I CAN'T.. I'M ....

THE HEAP CLUMSILY CRAWLS UP TOWARD THE HIGH WIRE AND... VON MUNCHEN!

HE'S GOING UP ON THAT WIRE TOO! - WHAT'LL I DO?

BUT THE HEAP WITH EXPERT BALANCE HAS GRIPPED THE MAN IN A TERRIBLE EMBRACE!!

OHH !!

GOLLY! THAT GUY MUST HAVE BEEN AN ACROBAT! HE'S LOOSE! BUT IF THAT MONSTER EVER GETS HIS PAWS ON HIM AGAIN...

LOOK OUT, MISTER! MAKE SURE YOU FALL ON HIM!

FOR A MOMENT, MAN, BOY AND BEAST WAVER ON THE WIRE...THEN THEIR BODIES PLUNGE TOWARD THE HARD STAGE!

AT THAT MOMENT..

THERE IT IS!! HEAVE THE TEAR GAS BOMB!! IT WON'T HURT THE KID.. ...GOOD THING YOU HEARD THE NOISE AT THE STAGE DOOR!

SEVERAL HOURS LATER...

YOU DID BETTER THAN VON MUNCHEN, RICKIE! THAT CREATURE STRANGLED HIM—AND GOT AWAY AGAIN, TOO!

IT'S A GOOD THING HE WAS UNDERNEATH WHEN I LANDED! BUT GOSH, CHIEF, HOW'RE WE GOING TO CATCH HIM?

AND MEANWHILE, IN AN UPTOWN APARTMENT, TWO MEN READ THE PAPERS...

VON MUNCHEN STRANGLED BY UNKNOWN MONSTER! HOLY PETE! DO YOU SUPPOSE HE REALLY SAW THAT THING?

I DON'T KNOW.. BUT I WISH WE HADN'T LAUGHED AT HIM! POOR GUY!

Daily Amer

THE HEAP

HERE'S A STORY THAT REALLY BEGAN IN A ROMANTIC GERMAN CASTLE LONG LONG AGO.....WHEN A LITTLE BOY DREAMED OF BEING A SOLDIER WHILE MILITARY HEELS CLICKED AND SWORDS FLASHED IN THE COURTYARD'S SUNLIGHT.....FOR THE LITTLE BOY WAS TO BE SHOT DOWN IN WORLD WAR #1.....AND BECAUSE HIS MIND REFUSED TO DIE, NATURE WAS TO TRANSFORM HIM INTO A SOGGY MONSTER KNOWN AS THE HEAP!!--AND NOW..

RICKIE RUSHES UP TO THE SOLDIER...

ARE YOU TOM'S FRIEND, THE ONE HE WAS HOLDING THE PACKAGE FOR?

YEAH...T-THE VON EMMELMAN PEARLS WERE IN THAT PACKAGE...I FOUND THEM IN A GERMAN CASTLE...I-I DIDN'T WANT ..TO BE CAUGHT CARRYING THEM.. SO I GAVE THEM TO TOM TO CARRY... I...

TAKE IT EASY! WHO WERE THOSE MEN? WHO HURT YOU?

"F-FOREFINGER".. THE RATHSKELLER ... YORKVILLE... OHHHHHH! AGHHHH!

THAT EVENING, RICKIE CARRYING THE MODEL OF BIRDIE, GOES TO YORKVILLE..

HERE'S THE RATHSKELLER! NOW TO GET TO THE BOTTOM OF THIS!

I'LL LET BIRDIE CIRCLE AROUND THE PLACE. I CAN WORK HER BY REMOTE CONTROL!

WHAT A DUMP! MAYBE I'D BETTER CALL THE POLICE AND TELL THEM WHERE I AM - JUST IN CASE!

AS RICKIE PAUSES IN THE DOORWAY AND LOOKS AROUND, HE IS SEEN BY MUTTON AND FOREFINGER WHO ARE IN ANOTHER ROOM...

HEY, FOREFINGER! IT'S THE KID THAT WE CLUBBED IN THE LOBSTER POT!

SO, MUTTON, WE'RE GOING TO LET THE KID HERE *WEAR* THE PEARLS SO THAT THEY'LL KEEP NICE AND SHINY— UNTIL WE'RE READY TO DISPOSE OF THEM!

ARE YOU NUTS, FORE-FINGER? YOU MEAN LET THE KID RUN AROUND WITH A HUNDRED THOUSAND G'S WORTH OF VON EMMELMAN PEARLS?

WHY MY DEAR FRIEND, WHO SAID ANYTHING ABOUT HIM RUNNING AROUND? WE'RE GOING TO BURY HIM... *ALIVE!*

A FEW HOURS LATER AT A WOODED SPOT OUTSIDE THE CITY...

YOU MIGHT BE A LITTLE UNCOMFORTABLE, KID, BUT DON'T WORRY. AS LONG AS YOU HAVE THOSE PEARLS AROUND YOUR NECK WE WANT YOU ALIVE!

THANKS!

THEY DIDN'T NOTICE MY REMOTE CONTROL BOX—AND THERE'S BIRDIE FLYING AROUND UP THERE! IF THEY UNTIE MY HANDS WHEN I'M IN THE CASKET I'LL STILL BE ABLE TO CONTROL HER!

OKAY, LET'S GET 'IM IN THE CASKET!

IN YOU GO, SONNY BOY!

AND I'LL WORK MYSELF OUT AGAIN!

EASY DOES IT, MUTTON! WE HAVE TO KEEP THE KID ALIVE!

BOY! WHAT AN IDEA! THE COPS WILL NEVER FIND THE PEARLS HERE! ONCE THEY FIND OUT THAT THE PEARLS ARE IN THIS COUNTRY EVERY FENCE WILL BE WATCHED!

YOU SURE ARE A GENIUS, FOREFINGER!

THAT'S VERY TRUE, MUTTON! C'MON, I'LL BUY YOU A DRINK IN THAT ROADHOUSE OVER THERE!

WHILE ON A MOUND OF EARTH A THIN PIPE PROTRUDES FOR AIR TO TRAVEL DOWN TO KEEP RICKIE WOOD ALIVE...

GOSH, THIS IS LIKE A MOVIE SERIAL! AT LEAST THEY FREED MY HANDS!

I'LL CIRCLE THAT MODEL OF BIRDIE ABOVE THE GROUND! SOMEBODY MIGHT SEE IT AND INVESTIGATE!

...THE MODEL BIRDIE CIRCLES ABOVE RICKIE'S LIVING GRAVE...AND THEN FROM ONE OF THE SURROUNDING BUSHES A GREAT SHAPELESS MASS TAKES FORM...THE HEAP!!!

IT WAS SWAMP VEGETATION MERGING WITH A DYING MAN'S WILL TO LIVE THAT PRODUCED THE HEAP!....AND THE STRONG-WILLED DYING MAN WAS THE GERMAN ACE, BARON VON EMMELMAN OF WORLD WAR #1.....

THE HEAP TREMBLES AS THE CIRCLING MODEL PLANE REVIVES ONE OF HIS FEW REMAINING MEMORIES...FLYING!!!

7

WHILE DOWN BELOW...

I'VE GOT TO TAKE IT EASY! I'LL HAVE TO WAIT A MINUTE BETWEEN YELLS OR I'LL LOSE MY VOICE!

AS RICKIE'S CRIES FOR HELP COME THROUGH THE AIR TUBE, THE HEAP STIFFENS AS RECOGNITION SEEPS THROUGH HIS DIM BRAIN...IT IS THE BOY WITH THE PLANE MODEL!

HELP!! HELP!

FOR THE HEAP ASSOCIATES ALL MODEL PLANES WITH RICKIE-WHOSE MODEL GERMAN FIGHTER PLANE FIRST ATTRACTED HIM...

THEN WITH PILE-DRIVER STROKES OF HIS MASSIVE ARMS, HE TEARS AT THE SOIL...

AND RICKIE IN HIS UNDERGROUND PRISON HEARS THE NOISE...

I HEAR DIGGING! YIPPEE! SOMEBODY'S DIGGING ME OUT!

THE HEAP QUICKLY GETS TO THE CASKET AND LIFTS OFF THE LID...

IT-IT'S THAT CREATURE!

SOON THE HEAP'S GREAT ARMS HOLD RICKIE IN THEIR PONDEROUS GRASP...

MY GOSH, WHAT'S HE GOING TO DO NOW?

BUT SUDDENLY THE HEAP'S EYES ARE RIVETED TO THE PEARLS AROUND RICKIE'S NECK!..THE VON EMMELMAN PEARLS! AND THE MEMORY OF HIS LIFE AS THE BARON VON EMMELMAN FLICKERS THROUGH HIS MIND!..

GOOD GOLLY! WHY IS HE STARING AT THESE PEARLS? LET GO OF ME!..YOU-YOU THING!

IN AN EFFORT TO DIVERT ATTENTION AWAY FROM THE PEARLS RICKIE SHOWS THE HEAP THE MODEL OF BIRDIE!..

LOOK AT THIS MODEL! THAT'S WHAT YOU WANT, ISN'T IT?

TORN BETWEEN TWO STRONG MEMORIES, THE HEAP FINALLY GRABS AT THE PLANE...

BOY! WHAT A CLOSE CALL! NOW I'VE GOT TO CALL THE POLICE QUICK! I'D BETTER MAKE FOR THAT ROAD-HOUSE OVER THERE!

BUT AS RICKIE RUNS INTO THE ROAD-HOUSE HE FACES MUTTON AND FORE-FINGER...

IT'S THE KID!

ULP!

BUT HOW COULD HE GET OUT, FOREFINGER?

SHUT UP AND GRAB HIM!

AS THE PAIR OVERPOWER RICKIE AND SNATCH THE PEARLS, MUTTON TURNS TO SEE THE HEAP ADVANCING TOWARDS THEM...

FOREFINGER! *LOOK!*

FOREFINGER! MAKE IT LET GO! MAKE IT STOP!

WITH BACKBREAKING FORCE THE TWO MEN ARE HURLED TO THE GROUND...

AND FROM HIS VICTIMS THE HEAP SNATCHES THE VON EMMELMAN PEARLS!

GOOD GOSH! NOW HE'S GOT THE PEARLS! MAYBE IF I ASK HIM FOR THEM, HE'LL GIVE THEM TO ME! HE NEVER REALLY TRIES TO HURT *ME!* HEY, YOU!...

JUMPIN' CATS! HE'S RUNNING AWAY! THIS IS THE FIRST TIME I EVER WANTED HIM TO STAY A MINUTE LONGER!

THE HEAP TURNS AND RUNS INTO THE WOODS.

LATER, AT POLICE HEADQUARTERS...

YES, CAPTAIN, THESE PEARLS IN THE PICTURE ARE THE ONES THAT CREATURE HAS!

HE MUST HAVE BEEN ATTRACTED TO THEM BECAUSE THEY ARE SHINY—FOR WHAT COULD AN INHUMAN MONSTER LIKE HIM WANT WITH THE *VON EMMELMAN PEARLS?*

PERHAPS IF THE CAPTAIN WERE TO SEE A SCENE IN A WOODED GLEN HE WOULD BE EVEN MORE PUZZLED—FOR THERE THE HEAP'S FIERCE EYES STUDY THE PEARLS—AND SOMEWHERE IN THE DARK REGIONS OF HIS MIND HE REALIZES THAT THEY BELONG TO HIM!...THE LAST REMAINING VON EMMELMAN!!!

THE HEAP

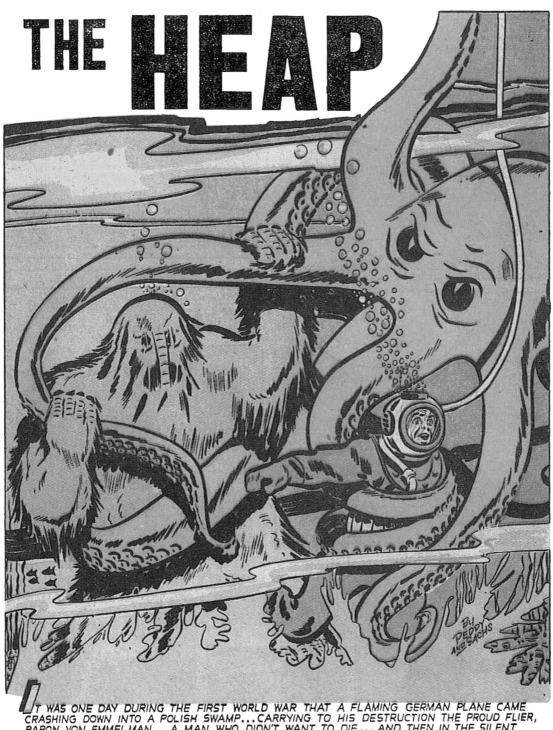

IT WAS ONE DAY DURING THE FIRST WORLD WAR THAT A FLAMING GERMAN PLANE CAME CRASHING DOWN INTO A POLISH SWAMP...CARRYING TO HIS DESTRUCTION THE PROUD FLIER, BARON VON EMMELMAN...A MAN WHO DIDN'T WANT TO DIE...AND THEN IN THE SILENT BOG THERE BEGAN THE WORLD'S STRANGEST TRANSFORMATION, BECAUSE THE BROKEN BODY HELD A **WILL** THAT FOUGHT FOR LIFE...AND TO THIS IN TIME NATURE ADDED A **MOCKERY** WHEN THE SWAMP'S VEGETATION BEGAN A HALF-WORLD CREATION THAT IS THE **HEAP** !...A SHAMBLING DEADLY THING THAT FOUND ITS WAY TO AMERICA AND BECAME ATTACHED TO THE BOY RICKIE WOOD BECAUSE OF HIS MODEL PLANE THAT CARRIED **GERMAN MARKINGS**...THE ONE THING THAT STIRS THE MEMORY OF THE HEAP.... **AND NOW** ....

ALONG NEW YORK'S WATERFRONT A FIGURE RUNS FOR HIS LIFE...

HE DASHES ON BOARD A FISHING SCHOONER AND..

MANUEL! WHAT IS IT? ARE YOU IN TROUBLE WITH THE POLICE AGAIN?

SHUT UP, COOKIE! WHERE IS ETHEL?

THERE SHE IS, NEAR THE BOAT AS USUAL!..MANUEL, HAVE YOU STOLEN THE JEWELS?

GET ME THE RAIL LADDER AND STOP TALKING!

A HALF HOUR LATER, THE POLICE HAVE COME ABOARD AND HAVE SEARCHED THE BOAT...

SEE! I TOLD YOU WE HAVE NO STOLEN JEWELS HERE!

I COULD HAVE SWORN YOU WERE THE GUY THEY DESCRIBED!

WELL HE DOESN'T HAVE THEM, CONKLIN, SO LET'S BE ON OUR WAY!

GO TO BED, COOKIE! TOMORROW THE AQUARIUM FISHER-MEN COME TO RENT THE BOAT FOR A WEEK-AND WE WILL HAVE PLENTY OF WORK TO DO!

YES, YES, MANUEL!

AH ETHEL! YOU FOLLOW MY BOAT AS ALWAYS-AND KEEP THE JEWELS SAFE FOR ME!

YOU ARE CRAZY TO TRUST THAT OCTOPUS, MANUEL!

HAVE SOME MORE GRIDDLE CAKES, RICKIE!

NO THANKS, MOTHER! I'M IN A RUSH THIS MORNING!

NEXT MORNING AT THE HOME OF RICKIE WOOD IN LAWNDALE...

I'M WORRIED ABOUT THAT HORRIBLE MONSTER! I'M SURE HE'S STILL IN THE WOODS! IF I COULD ONLY GET HIM INTO THE HANDS OF THE POLICE SO THAT HE COULDN'T HARM ANYBODY AGAIN!

FOR SOME REASON HE LOVES AIRPLANES! MAYBE IF I TAKE THIS MODEL DOWN NEAR THE BEACH AT THE EDGE OF THE WOODS, HE'LL COME OUT!

AS RICKIE FLIES HIS REMOTE CONTROL MODEL AIRPLANE, A SHAGGY FORM STUMBLES OUT OF THE WOODS...

OH GEE! HE'S COMING AS HE ALWAYS DOES! FOR SOME REASON HE NEVER HURTS ME - BUT YOU CAN NEVER TELL WHEN HE'LL TURN ON ME! I'LL *HAVE* TO GO THROUGH WITH THIS ANYWAY!

THIS MODEL CAN FLY FOR HALF A MILE AND THAT SHOULD CARRY IT WELL OUT OVER THE OCEAN! IF THIS CREATURE FOLLOWS IT, THEN HE'LL SINK AND THE WORLD WILL BE RID OF HIM!

CAREFULLY RICKIE RELEASES HIS MODEL FOR THE HEAP TO FOLLOW...

THAT'S RIGHT! GO AFTER IT, YOU BEAST!

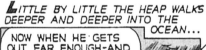

LITTLE BY LITTLE THE HEAP WALKS DEEPER AND DEEPER INTO THE OCEAN...

NOW WHEN HE GETS OUT FAR ENOUGH—AND *IF* HE CAN'T SWIM HE'LL JUST SINK TO THE BOTTOM!

THERE HE GOES BENEATH THE WATER AND I HOPE THAT'S THE LAST I SEE OF HIM! GEE, I WONDER IF HE CAN EXIST FROM THE WATER'S OXYGEN ...I HOPE NOT!

A FEW MINUTES LATER, RICKIE IS HAILED BY A GIRL IN A SAILBOAT...

HI, RICKIE! WANT TO GO FOR A SAIL?

HI'YA, WINNIE! THAT'S A SWELL IDEA!

IT'S SUCH A NICE DAY! I THOUGHT I'D JUST DRIFT AROUND!

SOUNDS KEEN, WINNIE!

OH, RICKIE! LOOK AT THAT SCHOONER! LET'S GO OUT TO IT!

I THINK THAT'S THE BOAT THAT THE AQUARIUM SOMETIMES USES TO CATCH FISH!

JUST A MOMENT, MANUEL! I'M RENTING THIS BOAT! LET THEM COME ABOARD!

THANKS, MISTER!

HELLO THERE! MAY WE COME ABOARD?

GET OUT OF HERE! I DON'T WANT ANY KIDS AROUND HERE!

I'M ROGER GARMEN AND THESE ARE MY COLLEAGUES, MR. BORDEN AND MR. CLARK!

HOW DO YOU DO.

HAVE YOU CAUGHT ANY FISH YET?

NOT YET–BUT WE'LL GET. THEM! YOU SEE, A LOT OF OUR FISH HAVE DIED AND WE'RE REFILLING OUR TANKS!

GOSH! HOW DO YOU CATCH THE SHARKS AND BIG FISH - WITHOUT HURTING THEM?

WE HAVE A HYPODERMIC NEEDLE IN OUR HARPOON! IT KNOCKS THE FISH OUT UNTIL WE GET IT IN OUR WATER TANKS!

BAH! WHAT FISHERMEN! I SHOW THEM ALL THE TRICKS AND THEY GET ALL THE CREDIT!

THEY GET THE MONEY TOO!

AH, HOW NICE IT WOULD BE IF "ETHEL" GOT HOLD OF THEM, EH, MANUEL?

YEAH! SHE WOULD MAKE SHORT WORK OF THEM!

CLARK IS GOING DOWN TO LOOK AROUND THE OCEAN FLOOR!

OH-THAT MUST BE FUN!

THE HEAP VICIOUSLY TEARS THE TENTACLES LOOSE AS THOUGH THEY WERE STRING...

BUT THE HEAP SUDDENLY FLICKS OUT A MAMMOTH ARM AND...

RICKIE RUNS TO THE STERN AND GRABS THE UNATTENDED WHEEL—AND WITH A HEAVE HE SPINS IT !!

THAT THREW WIND IN THE SAILS ! I'LL PUT HER ON HER SIDE NOW—AND THEN THERE'LL BE SOME ACTION !

THE WIND HAS SENT THE BIG BOOM CRASHING AROUND, SMASHING AGAINST THE HEAP AND TUMBLING HIM OVERBOARD...

WHEN RICKIE AND GARMEN GO OVER TO THE DEAD OCTOPUS, THEY SEE...

GOLLY ! LOOK ! DIAMONDS ARE DROPPING OUT OF THE OCTOPUS !

THERE WAS A JEWEL ROBBERY THIS WEEK ! MANUEL MUST HAVE DONE IT—AND ATTACHED THE GEMS TO HIS PET TO KEEP THEM SAFE !

BUT THAT OTHER THING ! IN ALL MY DAYS I NEVER SAW ANYTHING LIKE IT ! IF WE COULD GET IT—BUT I GUESS IT'S DEAD BY THIS TIME !

NOT THAT THING, MR. GARMEN ! NOTHING CAN STOP IT !

HOW DO YOU KNOW SO MUCH ABOUT IT, RICKIE ?

THAT'S A LONG STORY, MR. GARMEN, AND I HAVE A FEELING IT ISN'T ENDED YET !

THE HEAP

IT'S A MOUNTAIN TOP THAT WEARS A FOOLISH MAN-MADE CROWN CALLED "HOTEL DISASTER"!... ITS PATRONS ARE THE UNLUCKY AND THOSE WHO WILL NOT LISTEN TO ADVICE!...AND TO ALL THIS IS ADDED THE STRANGE HALF-WORLD CREATURE, THE **HEAP**...A PRANK OF NATURE THAT IS NEITHER PLANT, ANIMAL, NOR MAN...BUT A NATURAL CREATION OF THE BODY OF A HALF-DEAD GERMAN FLIER MERGED WITH A SWAMP'S VEGETATION IN WORLD WAR #1....AND NOW IN AMERICA THIS STRANGE CREATURE IS DRAWN TO THE BOY, RICKIE WOOD...ALL BECAUSE RICKIE OWNS A MODEL PLANE WITH THE FAMILIAR GERMAN MARKINGS....BUT RIGHT NOW LET'S CONSIDER THE FOLLOWING....

SOME MEN COLLECT STAMPS, OTHERS HOARD ART TREASURES - BUT MILLIONAIRE FELIX TIBBETS' HOBBY WAS... DANGER...

AS YOUR ATTORNEY, MR. TIBBETS, I MUST ADVISE YOU AGAINST CLOSING THIS DEAL FOR THE HOTEL ON MYSTERY MOUNTAIN!

BOSH! IF I LISTENED TO YOU, DOBBS, I'D NEVER HAVE ANY FUN AND I'D PROBABLY BE POOR TOO!

I REALIZE YOUR ADVENTUROUS SPIRIT AND THAT MOST OF YOUR SCHEMES HAVE WORKED, BUT THIS IS DIFFERENT! PAYING FIVE MILLION DOLLARS FOR A MOUNTAIN WITH A *JINXED* HOTEL ON IT IS PREPOSTEROUS!

NO MORE OF THIS IDLE CHATTER, DOBBS! GIVE ME THAT PAPER!

NOW THAT I'VE SIGNED THE OWNERSHIP PAPERS, I'M GOING TO FLY UP TO MYSTERY MOUNTAIN WITH ITS *HOTEL DISASTER!*

LATER AT HOTEL DISASTER...

WELL, MR. TIBBETS, IT'S YOUR FUNERAL, BUT I'LL SHOW YOU AROUND IF YOU LIKE!

ALRIGHT, MEN! START SURVEYING THIS BUGABOO! I WANT TO FIND OUT HOW SOON I CAN MAKE A RESORT PARADISE OUT OF IT!

YES, SIR!

THAT STAIRCASE IS GOLD GILT! COST A HALF MILLION BUCKS AND LEADS TO THE SWIMMING POOL ON THE ROOF!

HMMMM!

EACH ROOM WAS SUPPOSED TO RENT FOR $75 A DAY WHEN IT FIRST OPENED!

IT L-LOOKS AS IF THE VINES HAVE STRANGLED HIM!

HMM..THIS PLACE NEVER CHANGES.

DON'T BE A SUPERSTITIOUS IDIOT! ANYONE MIGHT FALL ON VINES AND BE CHOKED LIKE THAT!

BUT AS THE MEN MOVE AWAY, THE FOLIAGE SUDDENLY STIRS.. IT'S THE SHAGGY, BLENDING FORM OF THE DREADFUL *HEAP!*

AND AS TIBBETS RETURNS TO THE HOTEL...

SHALL I WIRE THE BOARD OF EDUCATION THAT WE WANT THE SCHOOL CHILDREN, MR. TIBBETS?

YES! YES! AND I'LL FIRE THE NEXT PERSON WHO BLABBERS ABOUT THIS SILLY FEAR NONSENSE AROUND HERE!

AT THAT MOMENT—IN THE TOWN OF LAWNDALE, A GIRL SHOUTS TO YOUNG RICKIE WOOD AS HE STANDS BESIDE HIS GLIDER...

HEY, RICKIE! HAVE YOU HEARD THE NEWS?

NO—WHAT?

OH, IT'S WONDERFUL! MR. TIBBETS IS INVITING OUR CLASS TO VACATION WITH HIM AT THIS NEW MOUNTAIN RESORT THAT HE OWNS! WON'T THAT BE SOMETHING?

AND HOW!! WHEN DO WE LEAVE?

DAY AFTER TOMORROW! THE SCHOOL BUS IS SUPPOSED TO TAKE US TO THE FOOT OF THE MOUNTAIN AND WE'RE TO HIKE UP THE REST OF THE WAY--BUT YOU AND I CAN DRIVE DOWN IN MY BOUNCING BETTY HERE!

OKAY-GOOD DEAL!

HEY—I'VE GOT AN IDEA! THAT MOUNTAIN ISN'T TOO FAR FROM HERE--WHY CAN'T WE FLY OVER IN MY GLIDER HERE?

DO YOU REALLY MEAN WE COULD GO THAT FAR IN A GLIDER?--AND COULD WE GET IT OFF THE GROUND SAFELY?

SURE!! WHAT DO YOU THINK A GLIDER IS FOR? AND NOW, ALL WE HAVE TO DO IS FIND OUT EXACTLY WHERE THE MOUNTAIN IS!

YOICKS! THIS IS GOING TO BE TRAVELING SUPER!

TWO DAYS LATER, JANE AND RICKIE ARE READY TO GO.

BE CAREFUL NOW, WON'T YOU, RICKIE?

I WILL, SIR!

'BYE, MOTHER AND DAD!

WE'RE OFF, JANE!!-- AND IT WAS A DILLY!! THAT WAS THE TOUGHEST PART OF THE TRIP!

OHHH—WE'RE UP SO HIGH! GEE, IT'S LIKE RIDING ON A CLOUD!

WHAT A SHIP! SHE GLIDES LIKE A LEAF!--NOW TO GET OUR BEARINGS!

YIPPEE-THERE SHE IS!--THERE'S THE MOUNTAIN--AND THERE'S THE HOTEL ON TOP!

THEN-AS THE GLIDER SWEEPS DOWN FOR A LANDING ON THE MOUNTAIN, TWO BEADY EYES PEER FROM BENEATH THE HEAP'S SHAGGY COAT...

THE STRANGE CREATURE THAT IS A COMBINATION OF MAN, ANIMAL AND PLANT NOW BLENDS WITH THE FOLIAGE AS IT WATCHES RICKIE AND JANE LEAVE THE GLIDER...

WITH ANIMAL CUNNING THE HEAP STAYS IN SECLUSION AS MEN RUSH UP TO GREET RICKIE AND JANE...

BOY! -- YOU KIDS ARE CERTAINLY ON THE BEAM -- FLYING UP HERE IN A GLIDER!

IT WAS FUN -- AND MUCH NICER THAN HIKING UP THIS MOUNTAIN FROM THE BUS!

MR. TIBBETS IS IN THE LOUNGE. I'LL SHOW YOU THE WAY.

THANKS.

WELL! WELL! WELL! MY FIRST SCHOOL GUESTS! AND YOU CERTAINLY CAME IN ADVENTUROUS FASHION!

IT WAS RICKIE'S IDEA, MR. TIBBETS!

YOU'RE PROBABLY FAMISHED...SO I HOPE YOU'LL ENJOY A GOOD SUPPER!

OH- YOU THINK OF EVERYTHING! YUMMY!

WE'D HAVE COME SOONER IF WE KNEW ABOUT *THIS*, MR. TIBBETS!

AND WHEN THE MEAL IS FINISHED...

THIS IS WHAT I CALL THE PERFECT START FOR A VACATION! AND NOW IF YOU'LL EXCUSE ME, MR. TIBBETS, I'D LIKE TO GO AND DO SOME UNPACKING!

CERTAINLY, JANE!

I KNOW WE'RE GOING TO HAVE A GRAND TIME HERE - AND I'M GOING TO GET A GOOD NIGHT'S SLEEP TOO - AND BE FIT AS A FIDDLE TOMORROW!

SMART GIRL!

MR. TIBBETS, I DIDN'T MENTION IT TO JANE - BUT WHAT'S ALL THIS TALK ABOUT THIS HOTEL BEING JINXED?

IT'S A LOT OF WILD POPPYCOCK! ...DON'T BELIEVE IT!

ONE HOUR LATER...

HERE ARE YOUR QUARTERS, RICKIE... AND DON'T YOU WORRY ABOUT A THING! THAT JINX TALK IS PURE BALONEY!

WELL-- OKAY...

BUT IN THE STILL HOURS, A MONSTROUS SHAGGY FORM FORCES THE OUTSIDE DOOR OF RICKIE'S ROOM...IT IS THE *HEAP!*

THE HEAP LUMBERS TO THE SLEEPING RICKIE.. A HAIRY PAW IS POISED ABOVE THE BOY'S HEAD ...BUT IN THE SOGGY MIND THERE STILL IS RESPECT FOR THE BOY WHO OWNS THE MODEL AIRPLANE WITH THE GERMAN MARKINGS...AND ONCE AGAIN THE BRUTE STOPS AT MURDER'S DOOR...

THEN RICKIE AWAKES WITH A START!

WHO'S THERE? WHAT IS IT??

WHEW!-- NOTHING HERE-- BUT I'D HAVE SWORN...

OH WELL-- PROBABLY THAT JINX STUFF WAS ON MY MIND--I HOPE JANE IS OKAY...

AND WITH THE LIGHTNESS OF A CAT, THE HEAP TAKES A LAST LOOK AT THE SLEEPING BOY AND SHAMBLES OUT INTO THE NIGHT...

NEXT MORNING - RICKIE AND JANE GO OUT WITH THE SURVEYOR...

WATCH YOUR STEP, KIDS--I DON'T WANT ANY ACCIDENTS.

WE'LL BE OKAY, MR. TIBBETS!

NOW...YOU TWO CAN DO THIS IN JUST A MOMENT...DON'T JAR THE TRIPOD...

STAY THERE -AND I'LL GO BACK HERE A DISTANCE--AND YOU CAN SIGHT ME...

OKAY, MR. STARK!

8

THE HEAP

THE HEAP IS NEITHER ANIMAL NOR MAN — BUT A HALF-WORLD CREATURE THAT IS A SAD PRODUCT OF WORLD WAR #1, WHEN THE BODY OF A HALF—DEAD GERMAN FLIER, BARON VON EMMELMAN, UNITED ITSELF WITH SWAMP VEGETATION..... AND IN THE PROCESS WAS CREATED THIS PLANT—LIKE THING THAT HAS THE POWER TO REMEMBER—IF NOT TO THINK VERY EFFICIENTLY..... AND NOW.....

FINALLY IN LATER YEARS, PAUL LUSTIG'S HYPNOTIC VOICE GAINED HIM EVEN FORBIDDEN PROPERTY...

BUT GREAT HEAVENS, MAN! THE PROPERTY YOU WANT TO BUY IS HALF THE TOWN OF LAWNDALE! I CAN'T SELL YOU THAT!

YOU WILL CHANGE THE DEEDS! YOU WILL MAKE ME SOLE OWNER OF THAT PROPERTY! I MUST AND WILL HAVE THAT LAND TO RETIRE ON!

I WILL HAVE THAT LAND! YOU WILL SELL ME THAT LAND!..DO YOU HEAR ME?

Y-YES, I-I WILL ARRANGE IT, MR. LUSTIG!

AND SO, HALF OF RICKIE WOOD'S HOME TOWN IS SOLD TO A...VOICE!

AH, INDEED! MY OWN LITTLE KINGDOM IN THE HEART OF A THRIVING TOWN! WORK WELL, MY MEN...THE WALL MUST BE HIGH!

YES SIR!

A FEW WEEKS LATER, RICKIE PASSES THE LUSTIG ESTATE...

GOSH, THAT LUSTIG ESTATE SURE TAKES UP A LOT OF LAND!

I HAVEN'T SEEN THE HEAP SINCE THAT HIGH WALL WENT UP! SAY! I'LL BET HE'S ENCLOSED THERE!! HE HID IN THOSE WOODS!

AFTER I TAKE WINNIE TO THE SHOW TONIGHT, I'LL GO BACK AND HAVE A TALK WITH LUSTIG! MAYBE THIS IS THE CHANCE TO TRAP THE HEAP WITHOUT ALARMING THE TOWN-FOLK!

LAWNDALE DRIVE SLOWLY

LAWNDALE OPERA HOUSE SHOW TONITE

THE HEAP

THE HEAP IS A MOCKERY OF NATURE... ....AND THIS HALF-WORLD CREATURE IS NEITHER ANIMAL NOR MAN — BUT THE AMAZING RESULT OF SWAMP GROWTH UNITING ITSELF WITH THE HALF-DEAD BODY OF A STRONG-WILLED GERMAN FLIER IN WORLD WAR 1......... AND VERY LITTLE IN THIS SHAMBLING CREATURE SUGGESTS ANYTHING OF THE FORMER BARON VON EMMELMAN....

Peddy & Sachs

AS OUR STORY OPENS, A SMALL GAUNT FIGURE SLITHERS ALONG THE WATERFRONT TO MEET TWO MEN.

HE IS GOING TO STAY AT THE MAJESTIC HOTEL! ONLY ONE MAN WITH HIM!

GOOD! HERE IS YOUR MONEY!

MAJESTIC HOTEL, CABBIE!

HE SHOULD ARRIVE ANY MOMENT! STILL, FELIX, I THINK IT ODD HE ISN'T GUARDED MORE!

PAH! HE IS ONLY A COUNT! COUNTS ARE CHEAP IN EUROPE TODAY, CHARLES!

NOT WITH EIGHT MILLION DOLLARS THEY AREN'T! QUIET! HE IS HERE!

A NICE LOOKING BOY, THIS VON EMMELMAN! WILL HE REGISTER UNDER HIS CORRECT NAME?

WHY NOT? WE MUST NOT BE HASTY, CHARLES! WE MUST THINK OUR NEXT MOVE OUT VERY CAREFULLY!

COUNT VON EMMELMAN AND HIS COMPANION GO UP TO THEIR SUITE..

YOU MAKE ME SICK, FRITZ! I DID NOT WANT TO COME TO SUCH A PLACE! I WANT TO SEE THE REAL AMERICA!

IS THAT SO?

YOU BLASTED WHIPPERSNAPPER! WHY DID YOU INTERFERE?

WHO ARE YOU? WHAT DO YOU KNOW ABOUT THAT THING YOU CALL THE HEAP? HOW DO YOU KNOW THE COUNT? ANSWER!

I KNOW NOTHING ABOUT THE COUNT! BUT I KNOW YOU LEFT HIM BACK THERE TO BE KILLED BY THE HEAP!

WELL, IT WAS AN UNFORTUNATE ACCIDENT, EH, MIKE?

OF COURSE IT WAS! THE *POOR* COUNT! HEH-HEH!

SUDDENLY...

FRITZ! LOOK!

IT DID NOT KILL HIM! IMPOSSIBLE!

FRITZ! RICKIE! GIVE ME A HAND! THIS THING THINKS I'M ITS *BABY!*

MEANWHILE, AT THE OFFICES OF DOCTOR STERLING, PSYCHOANALYST...

I TELL YA I CAN'T STAND PLANES! EVEN BEING NEAR THEM GIVES ME THE SHIVERS! WHAT'S THE STORY, DOCTOR?

MR. KISKA, PSYCHOANALYSIS REQUIRES TIME AND PATIENCE! IT MAY BE MONTHS BEFORE WE DISCOVER THE CAUSE FOR YOUR FEAR OF AIRPLANES!

WELL, I CAN'T WAIT MONTHS! I GOTTA FIND OUT RIGHT AWAY ...TODAY!

NOW JUST RELAX. THINK BACK TO YOUR CHILDHOOD. TRY TO TELL ME EVERYTHING!

HOURS PASS BY AND LITTLE BY LITTLE KISKA'S PAST COMES BACK TO HIM.. THEN SUDDENLY HIS EYES SNAP OPEN IN HORROR ...

DOC! I JUST GOT IT! I REMEMBER NOW... A WALKING TREE... WHEN I WAS A KID! I-IT WAS HAIRY AND ALIVE!

ER.. A LIVING TREE?

IT WAS DURING WORLD WAR I... I WAS A YOUNG KID IN EUROPE AND I WAS WALKING BY A SWAMP!

"YEAH, THAT WAS IT! AND RIGHT IN THE MIDDLE OF THE SWAMP, I SAW IT..."

G-GOSH! A GERMAN PLANE!

"I WAS WONDERING WHAT HAD HAPPENED TO THE PILOT, WHEN SUDDENLY I SAW IT!"

IT SEEMED TO COME RIGHT OUT OF THE PLANE! A-A WALKING TREE! I DIDN'T TELL ANYONE BECAUSE THEY WOULDN'T BELIEVE IT! BUT I SAW IT WITH MY OWN EYES!

NOW, NOW, MR. KISKA! CALM YOURSELF!

MR. KISKA, I MAY HAVE AN IDEA! NOW - IF YOU COULD GET SOME YOUNG MAN - ABOUT THE AGE *YOU* WERE WHEN THIS HAPPENED, AND TAKE THIS YOUNG MAN BY THE HAND AND GO TO A SWAMPY SPOT SUCH AS THE ONE OF YOUR BOYHOOD..

I GET IT! -- YOU MEAN TO TRY TO GO THROUGH THE *SAME MOTIONS* I DID AS A KID -- AND IT WOULD WIPE THE FEAR OUT OF MY MIND?

YES -- I MUST SAY THAT IT'S ONE OF THE MOST FANTASTIC CAUSES I'VE ENCOUNTERED, MR. KISKA -- AND SO IRONIC THAT YOUR POSITION SHOULD BECOME WHAT IT IS IN THE AVIATION WORLD!

DON'T *YOU* WORRY TOO MUCH ABOUT MY POSITION BEING WHAT IT IS, DOC...

HERE -- JUST SO'S YOU *DON'T* WORRY -- AND BE INCLINED TO TELL STORIES OUT OF SCHOOL ABOUT HOW JOE KISKA THINKS HE SEES WALKIN' TREES...

BAM!

I CAN SEE IT NOW...THAT TREE ...WALKING LIKE A MAN...

HELLO, BOSS! SAY, THAT NEW GUY, YOST, IS IN YOUR OFFICE! HE'S GOT SOMETHING IMPORTANT TO SEE YA ABOUT..HE SAYS!

YEAH?

KISKA, I GOT A MILLION BUCKS WORTH OF NEWS! I FOUND IT...THE *HEAP* HIMSELF!

WHAT ARE YA TALKING ABOUT?

RIGHT HERE! THE MONSTER EVERY COP IN THE STATE IS LOOKING FOR! THE THING'S HOLED UP RIGHT IN THE SWAMP LANDING STRIP! I SAW IT MYSELF..LIKE A SHAGGY WALKING TREE!

WHAT?

5

151

JANIE DIDN'T TELL ME WHAT YOU PLANNED TO HUNT, MR. KISKA.

EH? OH, A FEW RABBITS... MAYBE A FOX OR SO!

MEANWHILE --- IN THE SWAMP NEAR LAWNDALE, *THE HEAP*, A COMBINATION OF THE DEAD FLIER BARON VON EMMELMAN AND A SWAMP'S GROWTH NOW SHAMBLES ALONG...

HE COMES ACROSS A LARGE CLEARING AND DECIDES TO INVESTIGATE... SUDDENLY THE SOUND OF AN APPROACHING AUTO COMES TO HIS EARS...

KEEP YOUR EYES OPEN, KID! I'VE GOT TO GET THAT THING! I'VE GOT TO-OR I'LL GO NUTS!

WHAT ARE YOU TALKING ABOUT, MR. KISKA?

ARE YOU SURE YOU FEEL WELL?

YES! YES! JUST WATCH FOR IT! YOU'VE GOT TO SEE IT- SO THAT I WILL BE FREE OF FEAR!

SUDDENLY, A DEAD BRANCH SNAPS BEHIND RICKIE AND KISKA!

LOOK! LOOK! THERE IT IS!

THE HEAP!

QUICK! INTO THE HANGAR!

B-BUT WHY WERE YOU *LOOKING* FOR THE HEAP?

THEN--A HALF-DEAD FIGURE WITH A GUN STUMBLES THROUGH THE DOOR!

THE HEAP

AT A FASHIONABLE BEACH RESORT...

FROM THE OLD MAN, EH? WHAT'S HE WANT NOW?

I DUNNO! JUST SAYS TO GET BACK AS SOON AS WE CAN!

I WONDER WHAT THE OLD COOT HAS IN MIND?

I SHOULD THINK HE'D BE TOO BUSY TO BOTHER US SINCE HE'S SO INTERESTED IN THAT GERMAN VON EMMELMAN CASTLE THAT HE HAD SHIPPED OVER HERE STONE BY STONE!

BUT—AS MR. TURNER STEPS FROM THE CURB TO CROSS THE STREET—A CAR BRAKE IS RELEASED!

THE DRIVERLESS CAR SPEEDS DOWN THE GRADE—RIGHT AT MR. TURNER!!

THE NEXT DAY WHEN THE VON EMMELMAN CASTLE IS SUPPOSED TO BE OPENED TO THE PUBLIC...

I'M SORRY, LADIES AND GENTLEMEN, BUT DUE TO MY POOR FATHER'S DEATH, WE WILL BE UNABLE TO OPEN THE CASTLE!

OH-H-H!

LISTEN, BILL! DON'T THINK I DON'T KNOW **WHO** RELEASED THE BRAKE ON THE CAR THAT KILLED DAD!

YOU'RE DARN RIGHT YOU KNOW! IT WAS *YOU*!

DON'T TRY TO FRAME ME, YOU HEEL!

SHUT UP, PAUL! WE CAN'T DO ANYTHING ABOUT IT NOW! THE MONEY IS OURS AT LAST!

MEANWHILE RICKIE WOOD AND HIS FRIEND, CONNIE DAWSON STAND IN FRONT OF THE CASTLE.

OH, RICKIE! I'M SO DISAPPOINTED! I WANTED TO SEE IT!

THEY'LL PROBABLY OPEN IT AFTER MR. TURNER'S FUNERAL, CONNIE!

CONNIE! LOOK OVER THERE! YOU MEAN THAT MAN GOING INTO THE CASTLE, RICKIE? HE'S BEEN HANGING AROUND SINCE WE'VE BEEN HERE! HE'S PROBABLY FROM TURNER'S STORE!

I DON'T MEAN *HIM!* I SAW SOMETHING MOVING IN THE BUSHES BEHIND HIM!

THE *HEAP!*

OH-H-H!

BUT AS RICKIE AND CONNIE GET ON THE DRAWBRIDGE, THE HEAP WITH HIS TREMENDOUS STRENGTH PULLS ON THE CHAINS SO HARD THAT HE SENDS THEM HURTLING THROUGH THE AIR!

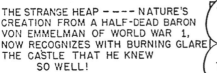

THE STRANGE HEAP — — — — NATURE'S CREATION FROM A HALF-DEAD BARON VON EMMELMAN OF WORLD WAR 1, NOW RECOGNIZES WITH BURNING GLARE THE CASTLE THAT HE KNEW SO WELL!

THAT THING'S A MENACE! IT'S GOING ACROSS THE DRAWBRIDGE! IF I CAN LOCK HIM IN THE CASTLE, THERE'LL BE TIME TO CALL THE POLICE!

OHHH!

WHAT THE..!

THEY LAND UNHURT ON A BALCONY...

HOW D'YA LIKE THAT!! — THAT MONSTER MUST HAVE THE STRENGTH OF *FIFTY* MEN!

SLOWLY THE HEAP LUMBERS THROUGH THE GREAT ROOMS THAT HE KNEW AS A BOY!

...WHILE IN ANOTHER SECTION, PAUL AND WILLIAM TURNER INSPECT THEIR NEW INHERITANCE...

I'M GOING TO LOOK IN THIS ROOM, PAUL! THE PAINTINGS MUST BE WORTH A FORTUNE!

OKAY, BILL! I'M GOING UP TO THE TOWER!

BUT A MINUTE AFTER BILL ENTERS THE ROOM, THE HEAP PASSES THE OPEN DOOR AND SLAMS IT SHUT...

SLAM!

HEY!

CLICK!

PAUL'S LOCKED ME IN! HE'S TRYING TO KILL ME-SO THAT HE CAN KEEP THE WHOLE FORTUNE!

THAT DOUBLE-CROSSING RAT! I EXPECTED SOMETHING LIKE THIS!

RICKIE AND CONNIE SEE BILL LEAVE THE ROOM BY A WINDOW!

RICKIE! THAT MAN HAS A GUN!

HE MUST BE AFTER THE HEAP TOO!

...AND HE WAITS FOR HIS BROTHER PAUL TO STEP ONTO THE PARAPET ABOVE...

NOT ONLY WILL I GET THE MONEY NOW, BUT I CAN PLEAD SELF-DEFENSE AGAINST A MURDERER, SINCE HE KILLED DAD!

BILL!

BAM!

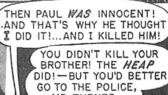

THE HEAP

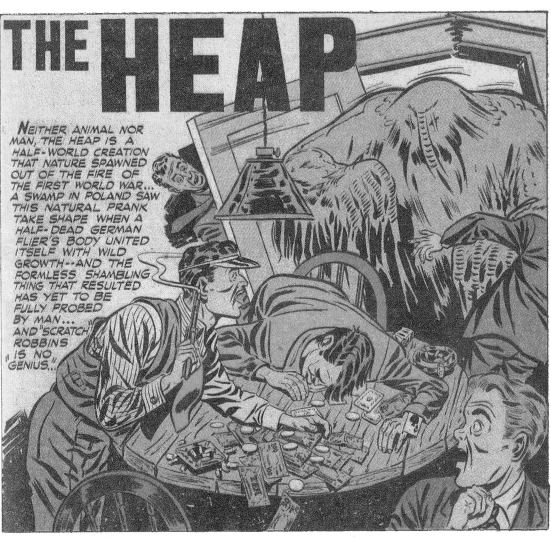

NEITHER ANIMAL NOR MAN, THE HEAP IS A HALF-WORLD CREATION THAT NATURE SPAWNED OUT OF THE FIRE OF THE FIRST WORLD WAR... A SWAMP IN POLAND SAW THIS NATURAL PRANK TAKE SHAPE WHEN A HALF-DEAD GERMAN FLIER'S BODY UNITED ITSELF WITH WILD GROWTH--AND THE FORMLESS SHAMBLING THING THAT RESULTED HAS YET TO BE FULLY PROBED BY MAN... AND "SCRATCH" ROBBINS IS NO GENIUS...

SCRATCH, HERE'S TEN GRAND I OWE "BIG BOB" MILLER! TAKE IT OVER THERE-- AND GET BACK QUICK!

SURE, MR. KEATS!

TEN GRAND! GEE! THAT'S A LOTTA LETTUCE!

A GUY LIKE ME COULD SPEND A LIFETIME EARNING THIS KINDA DOUGH! HMM... THE "2 BY 4" CLUB! I HEAR THEY GOT AN HONEST ROULETTE WHEEL IN THERE. NOW, IF I COULD DOUBLE THIS DOUGH BEFORE I GET TO BOB MILLER...

2 by 4 club

AND SOON SCRATCH IS PLAYING THE WHEEL...

28 BLACK!

RED'S GOTTA COME UP SOON! TWO MORE GRAND ON **RED**, CHARLIE!

WHERE DID YOU GET ALL THE FISH, SCRATCH? BEEN ROBBING BANKS?

SHUT UP! I HIT THE HORSES! A LITTLE GUY'S GOT A RIGHT TA WIN ONCE IN A WHILE, AIN'T HE?

42 BLACK! YOU LOSE AGAIN, SCRATCH!

JEEPS! ONLY **THREE** GRAND LEFT! RED'S GOTTA COME UP...I'LL LAY IT ALL DOWN!

LATER...

BUSTED! THE WHOLE TEN THOUSAND THAT I WAS SUPPOSED TO GIVE MILLER! KEATS'LL KNOCK ME OFF FOR THIS! WHY DID I TAKE A CHANCE ON GAMBLIN'!

2 by 4 Club GALS!

UHH?? WHAT GIVES...

HEY, SCRATCH!

WHAT'S THE MATTER? GOT THE JUMPS, SCRATCH? I JUST WANTA TELL YA KEATS IS WAITING FER YA TA GET BACK...PROBABLY GOT A JOB FER YA...

T-THANKS! I-I'LL SEE HIM RIGHT AWAY!

HE'S **GUNNIN'** FOR ME ALREADY! I GOTTA GET **AWAY!**

I'LL BEAT IT OUTA TOWN! HE WON'T BE ABLE TO TAIL ME...NOT IN THIS **STOLEN** CAR!

LATER AS SCRATCH APPROACHES LAWNDALE, HE PULLS TO A STOP AND TALKS TO YOUNG RICKIE WOOD...

HEY, JUNIOR! WHERE'S A HOTEL IN THIS TOWN?

THE ONLY HOTEL IS BEING FIXED OVER, MISTER, AND THEY'RE NOT TAKING ANY GUESTS!

I GOTTA FIND A PLACE TO STOP AWHILE! Y'SEE - I'M SICK!

SICK?

GOSH, MISTER, MY NAME'S RICKIE WOOD-AND IF YOU WANT, YOU CAN COME TO MY HOUSE! I'LL CALL THE DOCTOR FOR YOU!

YOUR HOUSE? YEAH! YEAH! THAT WOULD BE SWELL!

GOOD PLACE TA HIDE AWAY... FOR AWHILE!

KEATS WILL NEVER FIND ME HERE IN THIS HICK'S HOUSE!

NEVER MIND THE DOC, RICKIE, ALL I NEED IS TA REST A BIT... SAY, ARE YOU ALL ALONE HERE?

YES! MY FOLKS ARE AWAY FOR THE WEEK-END!

HERE'S FIVE BUCKS FOR ROOM RENT, KID! JUST LET ME STAY OVERNIGHT! I DON'T WANTA DRIVE NO MORE TODAY!

OH, I DON'T WANT THE MONEY! I GUESS IT'S ALRIGHT IF YOU STAY OVER!

THAT NIGHT...

THIS WAS A BREAK! I'LL HOLE UP HERE OVER THE WEEKEND...THEN DUCK OUTTA THIS STATE MONDAY MORNING!

SUDDENLY!!--SCRATCH IS JOLTED BY A FORM AT THE WINDOW!

WHAT TH'...!!!

3

165

HERE WE GO...I'VE SET THE CONTROLS SO THAT SHE'LL CIRCLE A FEW TIMES, THEN FLY RIGHT INTO THE OPEN BACK OF YOUR TRUCK!

THIS BETTER WORK!

THIS BETTER BE *GOOD* FOR *YOUR* SAKE, SCRATCH! I'M IN NO MOOD FOR GAGS!

IT'LL WORK — I BET'CHA IT'LL WORK! C'MON PLANE!

IN THE WOODS, THE UNDER-BRUSH STIRS — FIERCE EYES PEER THROUGH SHAGGY HAIR AT THE CIRCLING MODEL PLANE! IT IS THE HEAP!

AND THEN!!

WOW!! WOTTA MONSTER!

IT WORKED! HE'S FOLLOWIN' THE MODEL!

QUICK!! LOCK THEM DOORS GOOD! WE'RE ROLLIN'!

WHAT?? THEY SPED OFF WITHOUT ME! I'D BETTER FOLLOW IN MY CAR — AND GOSH....I DIDN'T NOTICE BEFORE—THAT'S AN ARMORED *BANK* TRUCK! WHERE DID *THEY* GET THAT?

KEATS, SCRATCH AND PETE RUN ONTO THE SUBWAY PLATFORM!

THERE HE IS! BLAST 'IM!

THE BULLETS ARE GOIN' RIGHT *THROUGH* HIM!

LOOK OUT! A TRAIN'S COMIN'!

HELP ME!! HELP ME!! HE'S CRUSHIN ME!

AND IN A MAD SCRAMBLE THE WHOLE GROUP TUMBLES TO THE TRACKS IN THE PATH OF THE TRAIN!

OHHHH! EEEK!

LATER..

IT'S KEATS AND TWO OF HIS GUYS - OR WHAT'S LEFT OF 'EM!

THEY MUST'VE HAD THAT NIGHTMARE IN THAT STOLEN ARMORED TRUCK -- THE POOR SCREWBALLS!

THE WITNESSES SAY THE TRAIN HIT THE HEAP AND THE GUNMEN!... YET THERE'S NO TRACE OF THE MONSTER AT ALL!

BUT IT COULDN'T HAVE ESCAPED THOSE WHEELS! IT *MUST* BE DEAD!

THIS IS WHERE I CAME IN, GENTLEMEN! ---I'VE HEARD THAT BEFORE!

7

169

KILL OR BE KILLED — *THE SURVIVAL OF THE FITTEST* — THESE ARE THE LAWS OF THE ANIMAL KINGDOM! THOSE WHO WERE STRONG, LIKE THE TITAN LION, AND THOSE WHO WERE CUNNING AND FLEET, LIKE MAN AND THE JACKAL --- THEY SURVIVED! THERE IS A SPARK OF LIFE, AN INBORN FIRE FOR SURVIVAL THAT HAS KEPT THE ANIMAL KINGDOM ALIVE, AND SHAPED ITS DESTINY THROUGH THE CENTURIES!

BUT THEN — THERE IS ANOTHER FORM OF LIFE — THE PLUNDERED PREY OF MAN AND ANIMAL — WHICH HAS SURVIVED — THE VEGETABLE KINGDOM! IN THEIR SILENT WAY THE THINGS THAT GROW FROM THE EARTH ARE AS STEADFAST AS TIME, FOREVER IMBEDDED IN THE GROUND THAT NURTURES THEM! THESE ARE CREATURES OF BEAUTY — AND WE WOULD LIKE TO BELIEVE THAT FROM THESE THINGS OF NATURE, A SYMBOL OF THE *GOOD OF THE EARTH* CAN COME TO LIFE AND WALK AMONGST MAN AND ANIMAL ON EQUAL FOOTING! AND PERHAPS THIS SYMBOL COULD BE KNOWN AS .....

THE HEAP

HERE, LET US GAZE BELOW! WE NOW LOOK IN ON THE YEAR ONE THOUSAND NINE HUNDRED AND SEVENTEEN, AS IT IS KNOWN ON EARTH — A YEAR WHEN MARS HAS HIS WILL!

AH YES! THE FIRST WORLD WAR! A *BEAUTIFUL* ERA!

BEHOLD THE LEADER OF THE GERMAN SQUADRON OF FLYING CHARIOTS! HIS FATE SHALL INTEREST *YOU*, CERES!

INTEREST ME? BUT SURELY THIS IS A MATTER FOR MARS?!!

"NO, IT'S A MATTER FOR *YOU*, CERES! THIS MAN IS AN ARDENT KILLER, A PROFESSIONAL SOLDIER WHOSE ONLY TWO LOVES ARE HIS COUNTRY AND WAR! MEN CALL HIM *BARON VON EMMELMAN!*"

HE LOVES WAR, AS HE LOVES FOOD AND LIFE ITSELF! HE IS THE SYMBOL OF ALL THAT *YOUR* PEACEFUL WORLD IS NOT! *BEHOLD!* HE IS STRUCK DOWN IN BATTLE!

BUT WHAT HAS THIS TO DO WITH MY REQUEST, O JUPITER?

THIS MAN IS YOUR KEY TO THE ANIMAL KINGDOM, CERES! IF YOUR WILL IS STRONG ENOUGH, YOU CAN LURE HIM INTO YOUR WORLD AND MAKE HIM ONE OF YOUR CREATURES!

BUT HE IS CONCEIVED IN EVIL! — HOW CAN I USE HIS BODY FOR GOOD?

WITNESS! HE HAS BEEN HURLED TO EARTH! IF YOU ARE STRONG ENOUGH TO FIGHT HIS EVIL, YOU CAN MERGE HIS BODY WITH YOUR VEGETATION AND MAKE HIM GROW AS A PLANT FROM THE EARTH!

HERE IS YOUR TEST! IF YOU *DO* MOULD THIS MAN OF EVIL INTO A THING TO FOLLOW THE LAWS OF NATURE AND BRING *GOOD* TO *EARTH*, THEN YOU SHALL PROVE MARS IS WRONG! THIS IS YOUR CHANCE TO SHAPE DESTINY, CERES!

IT SHALL BE DONE AS MY NAME IS *CERES, GODDESS OF THE EARTH!*

MY PATIENCE WILL WORK ON YOU, O HEAP OF A MAN, UNTIL YOU TAKE ROOT IN THE EARTH AND TAKE FOOD AND LIFE FROM IT! THEN YOU SHALL BE MINE! **YOU SHALL BE MINE!**

IT IS COMING, AS THE RAINS MUST COME IN SPRING... YOU HAVE TAKEN ROOT IN THE SOIL, AND YOU ARE GROWING AS A STURDY OAK! YOU SHALL BE MY SUBJECT ON EARTH TO WALK IN THE ANIMAL KINGDOM AND BRING IT THE GOOD OF NATURE! SO IT SHALL BE!

AND SO IT IS! **YOU HAVE COME TO BE, O HEAP** ...AND YOU ARE MINE!

AND SO THE HEAP WAS BORN... A THING OF THE EARTH, WITH THE MIND OF A MAN! IN THE YEARS THAT HAVE PASSED SINCE THIS DAY OF CREATION IN THE SWAMPS OF POLAND, THE HEAP HAS BECOME FEARED THE WORLD AROUND! FOR CERES' WILL HAS NOT YET COMPLETELY CHANGED THE TRACE OF THE WARRIOR'S MIND IN THE HEAP! THERE IS STILL A SHADOW OF LOVE FOR HIS COUNTRY, GERMANY, AND A MEMORY OF WAR THAT HAS YET TO BE ERASED! FOR THE HEAP HAS BEEN UNDER THE SPELL OF A GERMAN MODEL PLANE OWNED BY A BOY NAMED RICKIE WOOD! AND CERES HAS YET TO BREAK THIS GRIP!

ALAS! DAY AFTER DAY HE SITS BY THIS HOUSE WHERE THE BOY WITH THE MODEL PLANE LIVES! BUT I MUST BE PATIENT — AND I WILL BREAK THIS EVIL ENCHANTMENT!

WHILE UPSTAIRS, IN THE HOUSE...

THAT'S THE KID'S ROOM, 'FINGERS'!.. AND THERE'S THE PLANE... GRAB IT!

3

OKAY, SAM, I GOT IT! THE KID NEVER EVEN STIRRED!

GOOD! LET'S GET TO THE CAR, QUICK! I SAW THE HEAP SITTIN' OUT IN BACK! HE'LL FOLLOW US WHEN HE SEES WE HAVE THE PLANE!

HERE HE COMES... IT'S WORKING! GET IN THAT CAR FAST! HURRY, CRIMP!

I'M COMIN', "FINGERS"! LOOK AT THAT THING! IF HE EVER GRABS US!...

IT IS THE PLANE AGAIN! IF I COULD BUT BREAK THIS SPELL...

WHEW...MADE IT! AND JUST IN TIME! I DON'T GET IT, SAM! WHAT'RE WE GOIN' THROUGH ALL THIS FOR? THERE MUST BE AN EASIER WAY TO CRACK A BANK!

I KNOW...BUT THIS IS MORE PERFECT...THEY'LL NEVER TRACE US!

IT'S A SNAP! ALL WE DO IS TOSS THIS MODEL PLANE INTO THE BANK WINDOW, AND THE HEAP'LL BREAK DOWN THE BARS TO GET IN AFTER IT... WHILE HE'S WRECKING THE JOINT, WE HAUL OFF WITH THE JACKPOT!

BOY! WHAT A TERRIFIC IDEA!

BUT, THAT'S NOT ALL, FINGERS! JOE, THAT NOSEY BROTHER-IN-LAW OF MINE, WILL BE ON NIGHT-WATCHMAN DUTY! HE'S BEEN SUSPECTING TOO MUCH SINCE I STARTED ASKING QUESTIONS ABOUT THE BANK LAYOUT! HE'S TOO HONEST TO SUIT ME—AND SURE TO TELL THE COPS ABOUT ME IF THE BANK IS CRACKED...

NOW I GET IT...IF THE HEAP GETS LOOSE IN THE BANK, HE'LL PROBABLY TEAR JOE TO PIECES... YOU'LL KILL TWO BIRDS WITH ONE STONE! HA, HA, HA!

HERE WE ARE... THE HEAP'S CLOSE BEHIND... OKAY, CRIMP... LET THAT PLANE GO...

OKAY...SAM... I'M WINDING HER UP...

CITY BANK

CRASH

THERE'S THE HEAP SMASHING THROUGH NOW! IT WORKED LIKE A CHARM! WE'LL SIT IN THE CAR TILL HE'S WRECKED THE JOINT!

4

AND INSIDE THE BANK, SAM'S BROTHER-IN-LAW JOE GASPS IN AWE AS...

HOLY SMOKES! THE *HEAP!* HOW'D HE EVER COME *HERE?* I'D BETTER SOUND THE ALARM BEFORE...

BUT, SUDDENLY THE HEAP'S MIGHTY PAW ACCIDENTLY CRASHES THE PLANE TO THE FLOOR AND THE GAS ENGINE BURSTS INTO FLAME.

JOE QUICKLY SEIZES AN OPPORTUNITY!

THE FIRE...HE'S AFRAID OF FIRE... WELL, HERE'S A HOT DISH FOR YOU, GRUESOME!

IN AGONIZING HORROR, THE HEAP CRASHES THROUGH THE BANK DOOR!

HEY! HE'S HEADED RIGHT FOR OUR CAR! LET'S GET OUT OF HERE—BUT *FAST!*

YEEOW! HE JUMPED ON THE CAR.. *IT'S ON FIRE!*

LOOK OUT! I CAN'T SEE!

WHEW! I GOT OUT JUST IN TIME! THAT BLAST FINISHED FINGERS AND CRIMP...

DO NOT WORRY, MY HEAP! I AM STILL WATCHING OVER YOU! I HAVE GUIDED YOUR BODY TO THIS PATCH OF GRASS NEAR THE STREET CURB...THE FLAME IS SMOTHERED! NOW TAKE ROOT AND DRINK STRENGTH FROM THE EARTH...

BRUISED AND BATTERED, SAM HEADS BACK FOR THE BANK...

OF ALL THE BLASTED LUCK! JOE MUST BE TO BLAME! HE'S SPOILED EVERYTHING... WELL, I'M GONNA FIX HIM!

5

HE'S BEEN A CURSE ON ME SINCE I MET HIM... I'LL KILL HIM... I'LL TEAR HIM APART WITH MY BARE HANDS...

THERE HE IS NOW... THE PUNK..."HONEST JOE"... HA! WELL, YOU WON'T BE SO HONEST MUCH LONGER, JOE...

I'M GONNA CHOKE THE BREATH OUTA YA...AND WATCH YOU SQUIRM... NOW... *NOW*...

NOT SO FAST, SAM! I'M NOT AS DUMB AS I LOOK! I SAW YOU JUMP OUT OF THAT CAR...I'VE BEEN WAITIN' FOR YOU! SO YOU WANTED TO KILL ME, EH?

YOU HATED ME ALL ALONG... EVER SINCE I MARRIED YOUR SISTER! YOU KNEW I SMELLED A RAT WHEN YOU ASKED TOO MANY QUESTIONS! WELL, WHY DO YOU THINK I KEPT MY MOUTH SHUT? WANTA KNOW?

TAKE IT EASY, JOE...YA GOT ME ALL WRONG ...HONEST!

HONEST! HA! THAT'S WHAT YOU ALWAYS CALLED ME, HUH? SUCKER! YOU PLAYED RIGHT INTO MY HANDS! I WAS WAITING FOR YOU TO CRACK THIS JOINT...ONLY *I'M* WALKING OUT WITH THE HAUL...I'M GOING TO BLOW YOUR BRAINS OUT, THEN SET OFF THE ALARM... BY THE TIME THE COPS GET HERE, I'LL HAVE HIDDEN A PILE OF DOUGH IN THAT EMPTY LOT DOWN THE BLOCK!

NO...NO, PLEASE, JOE!

BEG, SUCKER...BUT WHEN THE COPS GET HERE, YOU'LL BE DEAD...I CAN SAY I TRIED TO STOP THE ROBBERY BUT ONE GUY GOT AWAY WITH SOME DOUGH... AND I'LL BE CLEAR... *ME*.. HONEST JOE... HA, HA, HA, HA!

NO, NO, JOE... YOU'RE KIDDIN...HEH, HEH! IT'S A JOKE... *YEAH-A JOKE! TELL ME, JOE! IT'S A JOKE!* ..YOU'RE *HONEST!*

SURE! IT'S A JOKE, SAM, AND *YOU'RE IT!* HA, HA, HA, HA, HO!

NO! NO! JO..OOOE!

NOW TO CRACK THIS VAULT... THEN SET OFF THE ALARM... WHAT A PERFECT SET-UP!

BOY! WOTTA HAUL... MAYBE HALF A MILLION... I'LL PLANT IT IN THIS LOT... HEY! THERE'S THE HEAP AND HE'S DEAD! I'LL HIDE THE DOUGH UNDER HIM!

SPREAD YOUR ROOTS AND GAIN *LIFE* AGAIN, MY HEAP... FEED! FEED WELL!

IF HE IN ANY WAY DESTROYS THE IRRIGATION SYSTEM THAT THE DESERT PEOPLE THRIVE ON, THEN I WILL WIN MY WAY— AND DESERT WARFARE WILL RAGE ON EARTH!

AND IF I GUIDE HIM OUT OF THE DESERT IN SAFETY, THEN YOU SHALL NEVER AGAIN INTERFERE IN HIS DESTINY—

SO BE IT! IT IS A WAGER!

CRASH!

AND SO, WITH A CRASH OF LIGHTNING, THE POWER OF THE GODS IS SET TO WORK-- AND THE HEAP FINDS HIMSELF IN THE WITHERING, DRY HEAT OF THE IRANIAN DESERT!!

TRAVEL ON OVER THE DESERT SANDS, O' HEAP AND I WILL SEE YOU TO SAFETY! DON'T GIVE UP... FOR WE CAN FIGHT WHATEVER EVIL MARS MAY CONTRIVE!

BUT MARS BRINGS EVIL IN MANY FORMS! AND NEARBY, AT THE HEADQUARTERS OF THE GOODWILL OIL COMPANY AT RAZAM.

ALF! THIS IS TERRIFIC NEWS! IT JUST CAME OVER THE SHORT WAVE!... THE HEAP'S OUT IN THE DESERT A FEW MILES FROM RAZAM!

YEAH!? SO WHAT'S SO TERRIFIC, TRECK?

STUPID... DON'TCHA KNOW? THE HEAP NEEDS WATER – LOTS OF WATER, SEE? NOW WE'VE GOT OUR IRRIGATION SYSTEM IN RAZAM! WHAT IF WE WERE TO GET THE HEAP INTO THE DITCHES!

WHY, THE WHOLE VALLEY WOULD GO WITHOUT WATER 'N' FOOD--AT'S WHAT! THE TRIBES WOULD BLOW THEIR STACKS!

EXACTLY! AND WE COULD BLAME IT ALL ON CHIEF OEHAB OF RAZAM! THE OTHER CHIEFS WOULD KILL OEHAB!

HEY! YOU'RE A TROUBLE-SHOOTER, TRECK! YER PAID TO KEEP PEACE! YOU KNOW OUR COMPANY LIKES THINGS ON THE UP-AND-UP! WOTSA IDEA?

JUST THIS: THIS IS OUR CHANCE TO MAKE OUR FORTUNE! IF "HONEST OEHAB" IS KNOCKED OFF, AND A DESERT WAR STARTS, WE CAN GET OUR HANDS ON THE RIGHTS TO **BLACK TASHMAL**, THE RICHEST OIL WELL IN TH' WORLD!! OEHAB WON'T MAKE A DEAL WITH US FOR IT, BUT THE DESERT TRIBES WILL!

SOUNDS GOOD! HOW DO WE DO IT?

LATER...

ACCORDING TO THIS MAP, THERE'S AN UNDERGROUND SPRING HERE!

RIGHT! WE DYNAMITE IT TO TH' SURFACE, AND THE HEAP'LL COME HERE FOR WATER!

...AND THIS SPRING IS AN **OUTLET** FROM THE IRRIGATION DITCHES! WHEN HE STARTS LAPPIN' UP THE WATER, THE TRIBES WILL SEE THAT THEIR WATER SUPPLY IS GOING—AND TROUBLE WILL POP!

I'VE LIT THE FUSE! SHE'LL BLOW UP IN A SEC!

BLAST IT! THIS STATUE GIVES ME TH' SHIVERIN' CREEPS! WHY'D YA GO AN' BUILD IT RIGHT ON BLACK TASHMAL?

STUPID! WHEN THE WELL STOPPED GIVIN' OIL, THE NATIVES WERE SEETHING...

SO I BUILT THAT UNICORN STATUE AS THE SYMBOL OF DESERT SWIFTNESS AND POWER! THE DESERT TRIBES WORSHIP THE SILLY THING!...NOW THEY CALL ME A GREAT MAN...HA!!

YEAH... HA!

SEVERAL HOURS LATER, THE STAGGERING, WITHERING HEAP REACHES THE SPRING THAT TRECK AND ALF BLASTED...

AT LAST, MY HEAP... **WATER!!** AND **NOT** IN THE IRRIGATION SYSTEM!

3

DRINK OF THE GOOD WATER, O'HEAP! AND I SHALL BRING YOU THROUGH THE DESERT WITHOUT HARM!

BUT UNKNOWINGLY, THE HEAP IS DRINKING THE WATER OF THE PRECIOUS IRRIGATION SYSTEM WHICH KEEPS THE NATIVES OF RAZAM ALIVE... AND WITHIN A FEW HOURS, THE NEWS REACHES CHIEF OEHAB AT HIS OASIS DWELLING....

GREAT OEHAB! A STRANGE CREATURE ... ONE THEY CALL THE HEAP... IS DESTROYING OUR SOURCE OF PRECIOUS WATER!

RUN AT ONCE FOR MR. TRECK! WE HAVE NO TIME TO LOSE! I WILL NEED HIS ADVICE!

WHAT'D I TELL YA, ALF? OEHAB WANTS ME AS ADVISOR! NOW RIDE TO THE DESERT CHIEFS AND TELL THEM THAT OEHAB PURPOSELY HAD THE HEAP DESTROY THE WATERING SYSTEM TO DRIVE THEM OFF THE LAND!

OKAY, TRECK! I'LL HAVE 'EM FIGHTING MAD IN NO TIME!

MR. TRECK! FOR YEARS OUR PEOPLE HAVE LOOKED TO YOU FOR GUIDANCE! NOW WE ARE IN GRAVE DANGER!

YES, OEHAB! I SUGGEST WE DO NOTHING IN HASTE! EVEN NOW MY AIDE IS DOING ALL HE CAN TO SETTLE THIS PROBLEM!

...AND MILES AWAY...

LISTEN, CHIEF! OEHAB DESTROYED YOUR WATER SUPPLY DELIBERATELY! YOU'RE NOT GOING TO LET HIM GET AWAY WITH IT, ARE YOU?

AHA, NO! WE WILL ARM AND FIGHT! AND WE WILL REWARD YOU WITH SOME RICH OIL GRANTS...AFTER WE'VE TAKEN OEHAB'S HEAD!

ARM, MEN OF THE DESERT! WE RIDE TO RAZAM!

YI-HI! DOWN WITH THE TYRANT OEHAB!

WITHIN A FEW SHORT HOURS, THE INSIDIOUS TONGUE OF ALF STIRS THE HEATED TEMPERAMENT OF THE DESERT CHIEFS, AND. THOUSANDS OF MOUNTED WARRIORS SLOWLY ENCIRCLE THE OASIS HEADQUARTERS OF CHIEF OEHAB ....

AND AT OEHAB'S CAMP...

OEHAB, GREAT CHIEF! THE DESERT TRIBES ARE ARMED AND PREPARED. TO ATTACK US!

SOUND THE TRUMPETS! WE WILL MOUNT AND MEET THEM ON THE FIELD OF BATTLE!

MEN OF RAZAM! — I HAVE STRIVED FOR PEACE! BUT FATE HAS STIRRED ANGER IN OUR LAND, AND WE MUST DEFEND OURSELVES AGAINST GREAT ODDS! LET US RIDE TO THE BATTLEFIELD!

AYAII! RIDE ON!

SOON...

CHARGE! DEATH TO OEHAB!

WE WILL FIGHT TO THE LAST MAN!

LOVELY! LOVELY! SO MARS HAS HIS WAY AGAIN?

DON'T LISTEN TO HIM! KILL HIM!

I AM A MAN OF PEACE, BUT IF I MUST...

OHHHH!

... I CAN KILL, TOO!

AAGHHH...!!

HOLD NOW, MEN OF THE DESERT! YOU HAVE BEEN TRICKED ... THE *HEAP* WAS LED TO A SPRING THAT'S AN OUTLET OF THE IRRIGATION SYSTEM ... IT WAS NOT *I* WHO TAMPERED WITH YOUR WATER SUPPLY! THE HEAP KNOCKED THE UNICORN STATUE OVER AND IT COVERED THE MOUTH OF THE *BLACK TASHMAL!*

EVEN NOW HE IS TOYING WITH IT! YOU SEE, BLACK TASHMAL NEVER WENT DRY! IT WAS *STUFFED UP* BY A *MAN!!* ...AND THE UNICORN WAS A DECOY TO KEEP US FROM DISTURBING IT! YOU ALL KNOW WHO BUILT THAT UNICORN ... *MR. TRECK!*

NO! IT'S A *LIE!*

YES... *YOU*, MR. TRECK! AND YOU INSTALLED THE MACHINERY TO OPEN THE WELL WHEN THE TIME WAS RIPE! THAT IS WHY YOU STARTED THIS DESERT WAR!

LOOK! THE HEAP! HE HAS OPENED THE WELL! IT IS TRUE!

NO! NO! STAY AWAY... IT'S NOT TRUE...I-I'M YOUR FRIEND! OEHAB'S LYING... *STAY AWAY!*

YOU TRICKED US! YOU MADE US WASTE BLOOD ON THE DESERT SANDS!

NO! YOU'LL NEVER TOUCH ME! YOU FILTHY... OOPS...

LOOK OUT! THE UNICORN!

AND, AS TRECK FALLS, THE LONG HORN OF THE PHONEY STATUE HE CREATED PIERCES HIS BODY! A CRY OF DEATH SHATTERS THE AIR!

HE WHO LIVES BY VIOLENCE MUST DIE A VIOLENT DEATH! SO IT IS!

AAIEEE

NOW PEACE MAY ONCE MORE REIGN, MY PEOPLE —AND PROSPERITY IS WITH US! WE MUST REWARD THE HEAP FOR BRINGING BACK THE OIL OF BLACK TASHMAL!

YES! WE WILL LEAD HIM TO THE SEA, FOR HE SEEMS NOT A CREATURE OF THE DESERT!

AND SO THE HEAP IS SENT DOWN THE RIVER IN A ROYAL BARGE TO THE FERTILE LANDS OF THE CASPIAN SEA... AND FREEDOM!

GRAZE IN PEACE, O' HEAP! YOU HAVE EARNED YOUR FREEDOM WELL, AND YOU WILL STAY FOREVER IN MY CARE!

...AND UP ABOVE, IN THE REALM OF THE GODS...

HO, MARS! GOD OF CONFLICT! MY CREATURE OF THE SOIL, THE HEAP, HAS OVERCOME YOUR DESTRUCTIVE INSTINCTS!

BUT ONLY FOR NOW ···AND I WILL YET PROVE HIM TO BE THE DESTROYER ·· HE IS NO DIFFERENT THAN THE REST!

THE END

THE HEAP

OFF LANGEEN, THE "ISLAND OF THE PEARLS" LIES THE TREASURE THAT HAS MADDENED COUNTLESS ADVENTURERS. EACH EYES THE OTHER FOR SOME SIGN THAT WILL SHOW SOME POSSIBLE ROUTE TO THIS KING'S RANSOM THAT THEY KNOW IS THERE IN THE WATERY DEPTHS. BUT THERE IS A PROBLEM, AND THE PROBLEM IS THE TREASURE'S "WATCHMAN"-- WHO CAN MAKE DEATH A FAR MORE UGLY THING THAN ANYTHING THAT CAN HAPPEN TO A MAN ON EARTH... AND BECAUSE THE HEAP IS HARDLY A MAN, IT SETS IN MOTION A GRIM DRAMA....

..AND NOW, CERES THE GODDESS OF ALL THAT GROWS FROM THE SOIL, OBSERVES THE HEAP-- THAT HALF-WORLD CREATURE THAT WAS BORN OF A DYING MAN'S STRONG WILL TO LIVE -- AND A CREATURE THAT IS THE RESULT OF NATURAL VEGETATION UNITING ITSELF WITH THE HALF-LIFELESS BODY OF A DOWNED FLIER ....

O, HEAP! SO LONG AS I HAVE MY POWER OF THE GODS, I WILL WATCH OVER AND PROTECT YOU -- AND SHOW YOU THE PATH OF PEACE AND GOODNESS ! YOU SHALL LEARN TO GUARD YOURSELF AGAINST ALL HAZARDS !

YOUR ONLY DANGER TO MAN LIES IN YOUR NEED OF FOOD -- FOR IN THIS WAY YOU DESTROY THE FERTILE LAND OF ITS USEFUL VEGETATION ... I WILL TAKE YOU TO A PEACEFUL ISLAND IN THE PACIFIC WHERE YOU MIGHT FIND ANOTHER SOURCE OF FOOD !

MAY YOU FIND REST, O HEAP, ON THIS COOL PEACEFUL ISLAND OF LANGEEN!

--- AND LATER, IN THE NATIVE VILLAGE ON THE ISLAND OF LANGEEN---

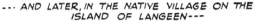

KING ONA KOONA! A STRANGE CREATURE LIKE A TREE DESTROYS OUR FERTILE LANDS!

WAIT, MY PEOPLE! THIS CREATURE MUST HAVE BEEN SENT BY THE GODS! WE CANNOT RISE AGAINST IT!

MEANWHILE ON A YACHT IN THE LAGOON---

YOU WERE RIGHT, TOLE! THE HEAP IS HERE—AND HE'S WRECKIN' THE WHOLE JOINT! BUT HOW DOES THAT FIT INTO YOUR PLANS?

I'VE BEEN WAITING FOR THIS CHANCE FOR YEARS, RAINIER!

WHAT'S YOUR ANGLE, TOLE?

I'M AFTER THE BLACK CHEST OF LANGEEN! IT HOLDS A FORTUNE IN PRICELESS BLACK PEARLS!

T-THAT'S CALLED THE CHEST OF DEATH! THE NATIVES'LL KILL YOU IF YOU GO LOOKING FOR IT!

NOT WITH THE HEAP'S HELP! COME ALONG, RAINIER! WE'RE GOING TO SEE KING ONA KOONA!

O, GREAT ONA KOONA! I BRING YOU GIFTS FROM THE GODS! THEY HAVE SPOKEN TO ME—AND I HAVE COME TO HELP YOU!

THE GODS ARE WISE! MY ISLAND IN GREAT DANGER! THE HEAP, GOD OF VENGEANCE, DESTROYS OUR LANDS!

OH, PRINCE OF FIRE, MAY YOU STOP THIS HEAP CREATURE FROM RUINING OUR CULTIVATED LANDS! ---

I WILL GO ALONE AND DESTROY THIS CREATURE!

LOOK! THERE'S THE HEAP! GET THE TORCHES, RAINIER!

HERE Y'ARE! IT'S A GOOD THING THE NATIVES DIDN'T FOLLOW! NOW THEY'LL BELIEVE ANYTHING WE TELL 'EM!

HERE! TAKE THESE BLASTED TORCHES AND BURN THAT HEAP TO THE GROUND!

WAIT A MINUTE, TOLE! I AIN'T NUTS! I DON'T WANT ANY PART OF THAT THING!

THE LONG SPURTING FLAMES DRIVE THE HEAP FRANTIC!

IF YOU WANT HALF OF THE PEARLS, DO WHAT I TELL YA! RUN THAT HEAP BACK TO THE JUNGLE!

OKAY, TOLE! BUT SOMEDAY YOU, WON'T HAVE ANYBODY TO DO YOUR DIRTY WORK!

HE'S GOING! IT WORKED! NOW TO GET THE BLACK PEARLS FROM THE CHIEF!

YOU'D BETTER WORK FAST! THAT HEAP MIGHT COME BACK AND THEN WE'LL BE IN FOR TROUBLE!

I RETURN, ONA KOONA! THE GOD OF FIRE HAS BEEN VICTORIOUS OVER THE GOD OF VENGEANCE!

WE ARE SAVED!

OUR LAND IS RESTORED!

YOU SHALL BE REWARDED, PRINCE TOLE! WE SHOW OUR GRATITUDE! ANYTHING YOU WISH SHALL BE GIVEN!

I HAVE SPOKEN WITH THE GODS! THE CHEST OF BLACK PEARLS SHOULD BE MINE AS A REWARD!

SO BE IT! THE GODS HAVE SPOKEN -- I MUST OBEY! WE GO TO THE FORBIDDEN POOL!

THE FOOLS! I'LL SOON BE THE RICHEST MAN IN THE WORLD!

YOU MEAN WE'LL BE THE RICHEST MEN IN THE WORLD.. .. DON'T FORGET THAT, TOLE!

SHORTLY, THE PROCESSION COMES TO A MAMMOTH POOL IN THE JUNGLE CLEARING!

THE CHEST OF BLACK DEATH LIES IN THE WATERS OF THE FORBIDDEN POOL BELOW!

AH! BEAUTIFUL BLACK PEARLS! B-BUT AN OCTOPUS! HOW CAN WE REACH THEM?

THE BLACK OCTOPUS HAS BEEN SENT BY THE GODS TO GUARD THE CHEST! IF YOU WANT THE PEARLS, IT IS FOR YOU TO FIND A WAY! OVERCOME THE OCTOPUS AND GET THEM!

WHAT? I, TOLE, DEMAND YOU SEND YOUR DIVERS DOWN FOR THEM!

5

... AND TOLE'S SCHEME TO PLUNDER THE NATIVES IS ENDED ---

MEANWHILE — IN THE DENSE JUNGLE, THE HEAP HAS SMOTHERED HIS BURNS IN THE WET GRASS...

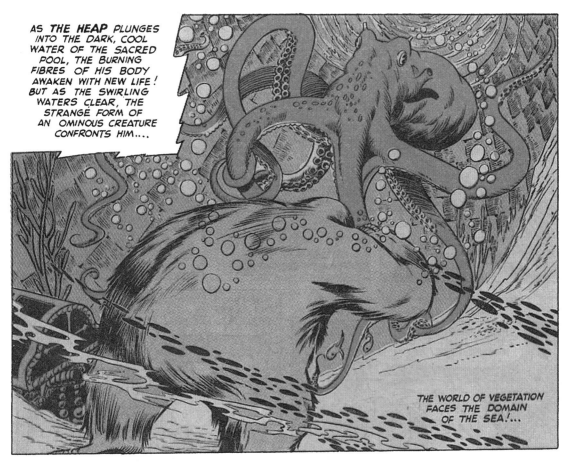

AS **THE HEAP** PLUNGES INTO THE DARK, COOL WATER OF THE SACRED POOL, THE BURNING FIBRES OF HIS BODY AWAKEN WITH NEW LIFE! BUT AS THE SWIRLING WATERS CLEAR, THE STRANGE FORM OF AN OMINOUS CREATURE CONFRONTS HIM....

THE WORLD OF VEGETATION FACES THE DOMAIN OF THE SEA!...

AND, AS IF BY SHEER INSTINCT, THE TWO GIANTS CLASH IN A STARK DEATH-STRUGGLE THAT SHAKES A VIOLENT CURRENT THROUGH THE STAGNANT WATER!

SLOWLY, RELENTLESSLY, THE SUCKING TENTACLES OF THE GIANT OCTOPUS ENCOMPASS THE THRASHING BODY OF THE HEAP, CHOKING AWAY HIS EBBING LIFE...

TIGHTER AND TIGHTER THE TENTACLES DRAW, AND THE DESPERATE HEAP SLASHES TO THE SURFACE IN A VAIN ATTEMPT TO FIND A VULNERABLE SPOT ON THE MAMMOTH MONSTER...

WITH A STROKE OF LUCK, THE HEAP PLUNGES HIS CLAW INTO THE SOFT FLESH BETWEEN THE DEVILFISH'S EYES—HIS ONE WEAK SPOT! LIMP WITH PAIN, THE OCTOPUS DESCENDS BELOW THE SURFACE AGAIN...

...PURSUING HIS ADVANTAGE, THE HEAP BITES DEEP INTO THE WOUND, DRAWING THE BLOOD OF THE SEA-DEMON... AN INKY SUBSTANCE BLURS THE WATER... AND THEN A RED FLOW...THE SIGN OF THE BATTLE'S END....

...AND THE HEAP EMERGES...SUCKING IN THE GOOD CLEAN AIR OF LIFE ... THE PRIZE OF THE VICTOR!

THE HEAP HAS BROKEN THE EVIL SPELL OVER OUR FORBIDDEN POOL! NOW THE PEARLS CAN BE RESTORED TO THE ALTAR OF PEACE!

THE GODS HAVE SMILED ON US!

LET US SEE THAT THE HEAP IS NEVER IN WANT OF FOOD AND WATER! HE WILL NOT NEED TO DESTROY OUR LANDS TO BE FED!

AGAIN, O'HEAP, YOU HAVE SHOWN MAN THAT HIS FEAR OF YOU COMES FROM WITHIN THE WARPED CAVERNS OF HIS OWN MIND! YOU HAVE SURVIVED THE JUNGLE—AND NOW YOU MUST GO ON TO MEET THE CHALLENGE OF OTHER PLACES!

THE END.

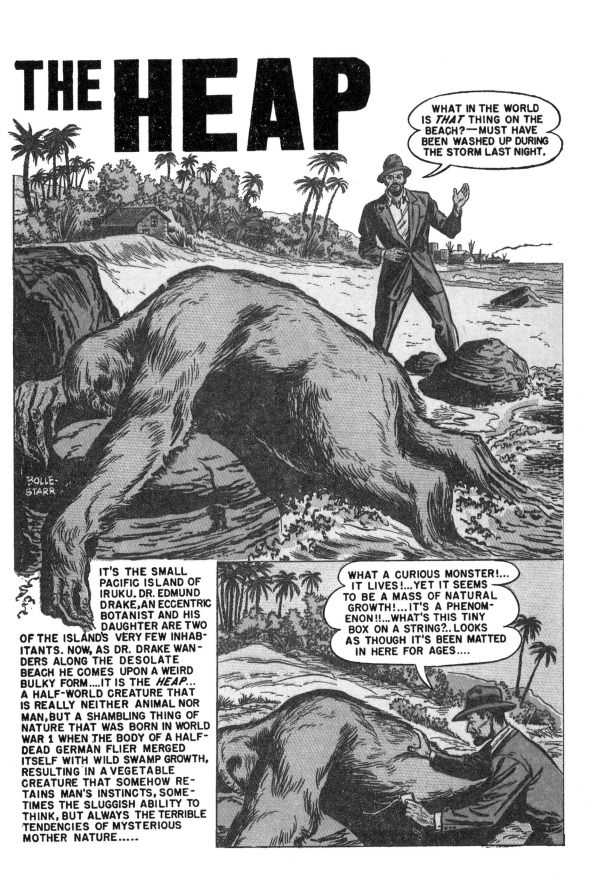

WHAT'S THIS?.. A MILITARY IDENTIFICATION PAPER IN THE BOX!.. IT'S GERMAN..."*BARON ULRICH VON EMMELMAN*".. SURELY THIS THING COULDN'T HAVE *EVER* BEEN A *HUMAN!*

SEVERAL DAYS LATER..DR. DRAKE ADDRESSES THE QUIET, SLUGGISH MONSTER IN A JOKING TONE OF VOICE....

WELL, VON EMMELMAN OLD BOY—FEELING A LITTLE BETTER NOW?

DR. DRAKE TIES THE HEAP TO HIS SMALL POWERFUL TRUCK AND DRAGS HIM TO HIS ISLAND HOME...

AT THE SOUND OF THE ALMOST FORGOTTEN NAME, THE HEAP STIRS WITH KINDLY FEELING FOR THE DOCTOR...

FATHER—I'M AFRAID OF THIS THING--WE DON'T EVEN KNOW WHAT IT IS, OR WHAT IT MIGHT DO!

I'M SO EXCITED ABOUT IT THAT I HAVEN'T TAKEN THE TIME TO WORRY ABOUT THAT! MY DEAR, YOU ARE BEHOLDING ONE OF THE WORLD'S PHENOMENA!

AND I'M SATISFIED THAT CONDITIONS ON THIS ISLAND AREN'T SATISFACTORY TO THIS THING'S EXISTENCE. IT NEEDS FOOD— AND SO FAR HAS MADE NO ATTEMPT HERE TO FIND IT.

WHAT DO YOU INTEND TO DO?

I HAVE A HUNCH THAT THIS THING'S MORE NATURAL HABITAT WOULD BE SOUTH AMERICA. AND SINCE THIS IS THE MOST IMPORTANT THING THAT HAS HAPPENED TO ME IN MY LIFETIME, WE'RE GOING TO TAKE IT TO SOUTH AMERICA!

THE FOLLOWING DAY...

CAREFUL WITH THOSE PLANTS, JOYCE—THEY'RE VERY PRECIOUS. WHILE YOU'RE DOING THAT, I'M GOING DOWN AND ARRANGE FOR OUR PASSAGE.

YES, DOCTOR! WE'LL CARRY THIS ANIMAL-LIKE CREATURE YOU SPEAK OF—PROVIDING YOU ASSURE US THAT YOU'LL TAKE ALL REASONABLE CARE TO PREVENT ANY UNTOWARD INCIDENT THAT THE THING MIGHT CAUSE.

THANKS VERY MUCH. I'LL TAKE ALL PROPER PRECAUTIONS DURING THE TRIP.

HERE ARE YOUR TICKETS, DOCTOR. YOUR SHIP IS THE "WHITECAP"...IT PUTS OUT OF HERE MONDAY.

SHIPPING CO.

WHAT CAN BE KEEPIN' THAT BLASTED RADIO MAN?

. NOT SO LOUD! HERE COMES "SPARKS" NOW.

SHIPPING CO.

WELL, WHAT'S THE WORD, SPARKS?

GOOD WORD! WE'RE CARRYING A CARGO OF DRUGS THIS TRIP, MR. ABLE!

FINE! THE MARKET IN DRUGS IS VERY HIGH NOW!

CAN WE GET JACK AND SLIM ON BOARD WITH US?

SURE! WE HAVE FORGED CREDENTIALS FOR THEM AS DECKHANDS.

THIS SIDE UP

...AND THEY'RE GOOD MEN, SIR — WE'VE WORKED WITH 'EM ON OTHER SHIPS.

WELL...THEIR PAPERS SEEM TO BE IN ORDER...

...AND I CAN CERTAINLY USE SOME ABLE-BODIED MEN. THE THIRD MATE WILL SHOW YOU MEN TO YOUR BERTHS.

YES SIR!

NICE WORK, BOYS!

THIS DRUG CARGO IS AS GOOD AS *OURS* NOW!

I'VE GOT THE LAUNCH ALL FIXED FOR THE GETAWAY!

AND BACK WITH DR. DRAKE AND HIS DAUGHTER...

WELL, WE'RE JUST ABOUT ALL READY TO GO, DEAR. OUR BIG FRIEND IS ALL CRATED UP AND SEEMS CONTENT ENOUGH.

THAT DR. DRAKE IS A SCREWBALL. DID'JA SEE THAT BIG THING HE'S GOT IN THE CRATE?

WHAT THE HECK IS IT? IT LOOKS LIKE A TREE STUMP WITH *LIFE!*

AND THE *HEAP* IS SWUNG ABOARD...

WELL, JOYCE — I HOPE EVERYTHING GOES WELL ON THIS TRIP!

I JUST HOPE THAT THAT MONSTER OF YOURS DOESN'T DECIDE TO HAVE A SAILOR FOR "LUNCH" SOME DAY!

THE LONG VOYAGE FINDS THE *WHITECAP* NEARING SOUTH AMERICA WHEN A TROPICAL STORM BREAKS!

THIS STORM IS OUR CHANCE—IT'S WORTH THE GAMBLE! MAYBE WE CAN MAKE IT TO LAND IN THE LAUNCH!

SURE! IT'S WORTH THE RISK—WE'LL GET A FORTUNE FOR THOSE DRUGS!

LET'S GO!

'MEANWHILE—JOYCE IS DOWN IN THE HOLD WITH HER FATHER...

I JUST HOPE THAT THIS STORM DOESN'T MAKE OUR BIG FRIEND ILL!

EVERYTHING'S SET. THE CREW'S BUSY—THE RADIO EQUIPMENT IS SMASHED!

OKAY—LET'S GET TO THE LAUNCH!

WE GOTTA SWING IT OVER FAST! IF THE CAPTAIN POPS UP, *PLUG* 'IM! — WE AIN'T GOT TIME FER TALK!

THE LAUNCH IS SWUNG FROM THE DAVITS...

C'MON, AL—DOWN AFTER THE DRUGS! STAY IN THE LAUNCH, SLIM—IF ANYBODY COMES, USE YER GUN!

RIGHT!

197

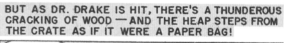

BUT AS DR. DRAKE IS HIT, THERE'S A THUNDEROUS CRACKING OF WOOD — AND THE HEAP STEPS FROM THE CRATE AS IF IT WERE A PAPER BAG!

AND NO WONDER! — BECAUSE THE HEAP IS ONLY VULNERABLE TO BULLETS IN THE SAME SENSE THAT A *TREE* WOULD BE!

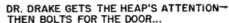

JUST THEN THE LISTING SHIP HITS A REEF!

ABANDON SHIP!

THE HEAP RUSHES BACK INTO THE HOLD AND GRASPS DR. DRAKE.

THEN JOYCE IS GRABBED AS SHE IS BEING WASHED DANGEROUSLY ABOUT THE DECK...

GOOD FOR THAT THING! — IT GOT THAT GIRL JUST IN TIME!

THE HEAP PLACES JOYCE AND THE DOCTOR IN A LIFEBOAT...

OHHH—WE OWE OUR LIVES TO THIS UNKNOWN THING!

LOOK! — IT'S USING ITS HUGE PAWS AS PADDLES!

AND SOON—ON A REMOTE PART OF THE VAST SOUTH AMERICAN COAST...

AH—THIS IS SOUTH AMERICA—AND UNLESS I'M MISTAKEN, THIS COUNTRY WILL PROVIDE YOU WITH ALL THOSE NATURAL THINGS THAT YOUR EXISTENCE DEMANDS, BIG FELLOW!

THANK GOODNESS!

BLESS YOU, BIG FRIEND! NOW I KNOW THAT WHATEVER YOU ARE, YOU HAVE THE HUMAN INSTINCTS OF A GRATEFUL MAN!

8

BUT *WILL* SOUTH AMERICA BE *GOOD* FOR THE HEAP?— WE'LL SEE—IN THE NEXT ISSUE...

THE HEAP IS A MOCKERY OF NATURE, BUT STRANGELY ENOUGH THIS HALF-WORLD CREATURE WAS ONCE A MAN— THE AMAZING RESULT OF SWAMP GROWTH UNITING ITSELF WITH THE HALF-DEAD BODY OF A STRONG-WILLED GERMAN FLIER RESULTED IN THIS SHAMBLING THING OF NATURE THAT BEARS LITTLE RESEMBLANCE TO THE DASHING BARON VON EMMELMAN... BUT THE HEAP SOMETIMES RESPONDS TO KINDNESS, AND DR. DRAKE, A NATURALIST, WHO FOUND IT ON A SOUTH PACIFIC ISLAND HAS GAINED THE MONSTER'S AFFECTION.... AND NOW IN SOUTH AMERICA THE HEAP HAS SUDDENLY SWEPT THE DOCTOR UP, AND IS DRAGGING HIM INTO THE JUNGLE....

THE HEAP

IN HEAVEN'S NAME, BIG FELLOW– WHERE ARE YOU DRAGGING ME?

THEN–DEEP IN THE JUNGLE THE HEAP COMES TO A SUDDEN STOP!

WELL, WHAT IS IT? WHAT WAS THE ....

GREAT SCOTT!! MAN-EATING PLANTS!... AND THAT MAN!.. THERE'S A DEAD MAN BEING DEVOURED BY THAT ONE!

YES!.. FOR THIS IS THE STRANGE BURIAL GROUND FOR CERTAIN PEOPLE!.. IN FACT THE AREA IS CALLED THE SACRED ACRE!.. AND A YOUNG WOMAN WEEPS AND IS COMFORTED BY A PADRE...

OH, PADRE–- WHAT SHALL I EVER DO WITHOUT MY DEAR GRANDFATHER?

COURAGE, ESTELLA...THE FINEST OF MEN MUST GO SOME-TIME... AND YOU MUST LIVE – AND MARRY... YOU WILL MEET YOUR OWN DON.. AND HE WILL HELP YOU RUN YOUR RANCHO!

HEAP! STOP! DON'T GO IN THERE! *STOP!* STOP!

WHY! THEY'RE BENDING AWAY FROM US!—THEY DON'T WANT TO TOUCH *YOU*, HEAP! THIS IS AMAZING!

THAT PROVES YOU'RE *CLOSER* TO PLANT LIFE THAN YOU ARE TO ANIMAL LIFE!—AND *NOW* WHAT ARE YOU DOING, BIG FELLOW?

HEAVENS!--HE'S IN A STUPOR-BUT LIKE A GREAT GREAT PLANT HE'S DRAWING NOURISHMENT FROM THE EARTH! THIS JUNGLE WAS THE PERFECT PLACE FOR THE POOR FELLOW!

...AND MEANWHILE... ESTELLA MARGUERITA LOPEZ-O'REILLY RIDES BACK TO HER HUGE RANCHO--HANDED DOWN TO HER FROM HER FATHER AND GRANDFATHER WHO WERE ADVENTUROUS IRISHMEN WHO MARRIED INTO OLD SPANISH FAMILIES...

MY SYMPATHIES, SEÑORITA ESTELLA!.. AND NOW THAT YOUR NOBLE GRANDFATHER IS GONE, YOU WILL SURELY.. ER.. BE IN NEED...ER. OF SOME *MAN* TO LOOK AFTER YOUR AFFAIRS ...AND I WAS THINKING..ER..

YES JUAN RODRIGO ALVAREZ ...I *KNOW* WHAT YOU WERE THINKING...

AND MY ANSWER IS *NO !!* -- I'VE HEARD OF YOUR BOAST THAT YOU WOULD MARRY ME AND BECOME MASTER OF MY RANCHO OVERNIGHT !

OUTRAGEOUS ! MY NAME IS VIOLATED ! OUCH ! DON'T *DO* THAT, SEÑORITA !

EASY, SEÑORITA, EASY ! WHAT A TEMPER YOU HAVE ! ARE YOU TRYING TO KILL THE MAN ?

PAH ! WHAT NERVE THAT OAF HAS ! WHEN A MAN TAKES *MY* HAND AND MY LANDS, HE'LL *BE A MAN !* MY HEART DOES *NOT* GO TO A SPONGE THAT WALKS LIKE A MAN !

AT THIS MOMENT -- A PLANE HAS LANDED NOT FAR FROM THE RANCHO...

THE MEN SKIRT THE AREA OF THE MAN-EATING PLANTS.

HEY ! I DON'T LIKE THIS ! IS *HIS* NAME O'REILLY OR IS IT LOPEZ ?

SHUT UP, MIKE ! AND THIS DELOS BETTER BE THE *REAL THING,* THAT'S ALL ! - I DIDN'T *FINANCE* THIS TRIP DOWN HERE FOR NOTHING !

DON'T WORRY -- *I'M THE REAL THING ALRIGHT !!* AND I'LL GET MY SHARE OF THIS PROPERTY !

I DON'T THINK THE HOUSE IS MUCH FARTHER FROM HERE...

HEY ! AM I NUTS OR D'YOU GUYS SEE WHAT I DO ??? ... *OVER THERE !*

AND NO WONDER ! -- BECAUSE THE HEAP IS AGAIN MOVING -- AND CARRYING DR. DRAKE !

TAKE IT EASY, BIG FELLOW - NOW WHERE ARE WE BOUND FOR ?

LOOKIT TH' SIZE OF THAT THING ! LEMME OUTA HERE !

SHUT UP ! ... JUST FOLLOW ME ... I KNOW THESE JUNGLES FROM THE TIME I WAS A KID !

AND TRUE TO HIS WORD, DELOS FROM CHICAGO LEADS THE MEN ON A PATH THAT TAKES THEM OUT OF THE JUNGLE...

WHAT TH' HECK *WAS* THAT THING, DELOS? YOU OUGHTA KNOW - YOU WAS A KID DOWN HERE!

DON'T ASK ME RIDDLES! -- HEY! -- THERE'S OUR LOPEZ-O'REILLY HOUSE NOW!

SEÑORITA, I HAVE BEEN WITH YOUR GRANDFATHER FOR MANY YEARS, AND NOW THAT HE IS GONE I WISH TO EXPRESS MY LOYALTY TO YOU...

YOU ARE A JEWEL, PABLO -- BUT *LOOK* - SOMEONE COMES!..

WELL! WELL! ...AND *YOU* MUST BE LITTLE ESTELLA -- ALL GROWN UP!

HMM.. I DON'T THINK I KNOW YOU!

I KNOW HIM, SEÑORITA -- HE'S YOUR COUSIN DELOS!

DELOS LOPEZ-O'REILLY! FIRST YOU BREAK YOUR GRANDFATHER'S HEART BY RUNNING OFF -- AND NOW YOU RETURN TO MAKE CLAIM TO HIS LANDS! WELL, GET OFF THE RANCHO -- AND NOW!

SMART GIRL! -- BUT YOU *HAVE* TO ADMIT THAT I'M A RIGHTFUL HEIR... AND YOU'RE NOT RUNNING ME OFF!

YOU HEARD WHAT THE SEÑORITA SAID!

AND IF YOU COME BACK HERE YOU'LL BE TARRED AND FEATHERED!

WE'LL *SEE* ABOUT THAT!

I WILL ALERT THE OTHERS ON THE RANCHO, PABLO -- THEY SHOULD KNOW THAT MISCHIEVOUS DELOS IS IN THE DISTRICT!

WHILE BACK AT THE SACRED ACRE...THE HEAP REFUSES TO LEAVE THE SPOT WITH DR DRAKE...

HE'S DETERMINED TO STAY HERE! -- AND I MUST GET HIM OUT -- PERHAPS IF I RUN A SHORT DISTANCE HE'LL FOLLOW TO PROTECT ME...

BUT DR. DRAKE RUNS ONTO THE LOPEZ-O'REILLY GROUNDS... AND AS HE SEES ESTELLA ON THE VERANDA, HE ADVANCES TO APOLOGIZE.....

I'M SORRY! HOPE I HAVEN'T INTRUDED, BUT I'VE JUST BEEN RUNNING FROM THAT PART OF THE JUNGLE WHERE THOSE MAN-EATING PLANTS ABOUND AND...

THE SACRED ACRE?..YOU WERE IN THERE AND YOU'RE ALIVE? YOU POOR MAN.. COME .. SIT DOWN AND REST...

AND SOON SEÑORITA LOPEZ-O'REILLY HEARS DR. DRAKE'S STORY...

BRRR!..THIS HEAP CREATURE OF YOURS GIVES ME THE CHILLS, DOCTOR! I DON'T KNOW WHETHER I'D WANT TO SEE HIM! ANYWAY, YOU MUST STAY AND DINE WITH ME!

YOU ARE VERY GRACIOUS, SEÑORITA!

I'M ONLY TOO DELIGHTED TO HAVE YOUR COMPANY...WHO'S THAT??

KNOCK KNOCK KNOCK

OH-SO IT'S YOU AGAIN!-- AND YOU TOO, DELOS!! WHAT IS THE MEANING OF THIS?

SEÑORITA! AS CONSTABLE I ORDER YOU TO ALLOW SEÑOR DELOS LOPEZ-O'REILLY TO REMAIN HERE! HIS RIGHT IS A LAWFUL ONE!! THIS PAPER PROVES THAT!

ALSO, ESTELLA-MY FRIENDS STAY TOO! THEY ARE MY GUESTS!

AS THEY SAY IN THE STATES, "SORT OF MUSCLING IN-TAKING THE JOINT OVER"... IS THAT IT, DELOS?

SEÑORITA...IF THERE IS ANYTHING I CAN DO...

I GUESS NOT! NOT AT THE MOMENT ANYWAY! MAYBE MY COUSIN IS WITHIN HIS LEGAL RIGHT!

BOY!– DIS IS SOME SWELL LAYOUT HERE, DELOS! YOU DIDN'T LIE!

WELL, KOTCH–NOW D'YA THINK THIS STAKE WILL PAY OFF MY GAMBLING DEBTS TO YOU?

LISTEN! YOU AIN'T GOT ANYTHING YET! I'M A LITTLE AFRAID OF THIS SMART-LOOKIN' PROFESSOR GUY!

DON'T WORRY! I'VE GOT AN IDEA HOW TO GET RID OF HIM –AND MY COUSIN ESTELLA TOO! C'MON ... NOW WE'LL OPEN THAT TRUNK I BROUGHT ALONG ... I'LL SHOW YOU SOMETHING!

SEE? HERE'S WHAT I MEAN.. THIS OLD *FILM!*.. AND TONIGHT, KIDDIES, WE'RE GOING TO SHOW A MOVIE!

I GET IT, DELOS-- AND IN THE DARK, ESTELLA AND THE PROFESSOR GET THE WORKS!

AND LATER...

LISTEN, ESTELLA-WHY CAN'T YOU FORGET YOUR BITTERNESS – FOR THE MOMENT ANYWAY! GRANDFATHER WOULDN'T WANT YOU TO TREAT ME LIKE THIS, WOULD HE?

YOU HAVE YOUR NERVE TO MENTION GRANDFATHER! LET'S JUST CONCENTRATE ON THE MOVIE FOR THE TIME BEING!

THEN OUT ON THE MOONLIT VERANDA...

REMEMBER, FRANKIE- DON'T LET *ANYBODY* INTERFERE WITH US! BUT DON'T USE THE TYPEWRITER UNLESS YOU *HAVE* TO!

OKAY, DELOS!

BUT AT THIS MOMENT IN THE DARKNESS, THE HEAP APPROACHES THE HOUSE...

OKAY, KOTCH — SNAP OFF THE LIGHTS!

RIGHT, DELOS!

NOW THESE WERE TAKEN IN 1915 JUST BEFORE SOME POLO MATCHES HERE IN THE ARGENTINE.. THAT'S ME IN THE HELMET... THE OTHER FELLOW WAS A GERMAN ... BARON ULRICH VON EMMELMAN...

BARON VON EMMELMAN! I'VE HEARD OF HIM.. HE WAS A BRILLIANT FLIER IN WORLD WAR I.. HE WAS SHOT DOWN IN ACTION...

AND THROUGH THE WINDOW THE HEAP WATCHES WITH ASTONISHED SURPRISE AS HE SEES HIS OWN YOUTHFUL IMAGE OF THE DASHING BARON VON EMMELMAN!

VON EMMELMAN CAME ALL THE WAY FROM GERMANY FOR THESE MATCHES... NOW WATCH... THE NEXT FEW SCENES ARE TERRIFIC!

THIS ACTION TOOK PLACE TOWARD THE END OF THE GAME... VON EMMELMAN WAS ABOUT TO SCORE THE WINNING GOAL FOR GERMANY... THAT'S ME RIDING RIGHT BEHIND HIM ...

OH-OH! I MADE A GOAL-- RIGHT ON VON EMMELMAN'S HEAD! -- AN "ACCIDENT" OF COURSE! THOSE THINGS WILL HAPPEN ...

ACCIDENT NOTHING! OF ALL THE DIRTY TRICKS!.. AND YOU PRACTICALLY BOAST OF IT!

SHUT UP!! THERE WAS NOTHING EVER PROVEN THAT IT WAS INTENTIONAL -- AND I'M NOT MAKING ANY APOLOGIES TO *YOU* IN MY *OWN HOUSE!*

YOUR HOUSE?? WELL, JUST FOR *THAT* I'LL SEE THAT YOU AND YOUR UGLY FRIENDS ARE THROWN OUT OF HERE *FAST!!*

NO YOU WON'T! OKAY, BOYS - C'MON IN - AND LET'S TAKE CARE OF THESE CHUMPS!

C'MON, SIS! - AN' YOU TOO, BALDY!

MAKE SURE HE AIN'T GOT A GUN!

BUT THE HEAP'S HUGE FORM APPEARS IN THE DOORWAY!

EEEEEEK! LOOK!

AND THE INTRUDERS ARE SWEPT UP INTO THE MASSIVE PAWS AND CRUSHED LIKE KITTENS!

IT'S KILLIN' ME!

SAVE US!

WITH AMAZING AGILITY THE HEAP PLUNGES FROM THE HOUSE WITH HIS STRUGGLING LOAD!

AND A FEW MINUTES LATER THEY ARE HURTLED INTO THE YAWNING JAWS OF THE MAN - EATING PLANTS IN THE SACRED ACRE!

AND BACK WITH DR. DRAKE AND ESTELLA ....

I WONDER WHERE THE HEAP DRAGGED THEM...SHALL WE ...

NO, DOCTOR - I'M NOT INTERESTED I ONLY WANT TO SIT DOWN - AND MAYBE BY THE TIME I'M 80 I'LL BE ABLE TO FORGET THIS DAY!

THE HEAP

To know how THE HEAP began we must go back to a swamp in Poland during World War I. Above the lonely swamp a vicious air battle between Allied and German planes takes place... One of the German fighters, Baron Von Emmelman is shot down... As his flaming plane hits the swamp his body is thrown clear of the wreckage--and there begins the world's strangest life and death struggle. Life ebbs from the body but the Baron's stubborn mind fights on for existence-- and there in the swamp nature steps in and adds her wild growth to create a thing that is neither animal nor man... Months pass, and this shapeless thing now rises to survey the world through a foggy mind and with a body that is just as invulnerable to injury as a tree would be! Out of man's design THE HEAP found its way to South America... But now we come upon it in a Costa Rican jungle...

GET BACK, YA CRAZY THING! WHAT *ARE* YA ANYWAY?? I'LL DRILL YA LIKE A SIEVE!

NO, NED--*NO!!* DON'T-- THAT THING AIN'T BAD I TELL YA! C'MON!

BUT THE MEN HAVE GONE SOME DISTANCE WHEN...

LOOK! HERE'S THAT THING AGAIN! THE SHOTS DIDN'T HURT IT A BIT! IT'S BEEN FOLLOWIN' US EVER SINCE YOU GAVE IT WATER!

WHATEVER IT IS, IT'S HARMLESS, NED! TH' THING GIVES ME THE CREEPS--IT SOMETIMES SEEMS LIKE IT'S TRYIN' TA TALK!

WELL, I'M TURNIN' IN FER TH' NIGHT, NED! AN' THAT CRITTER WON'T BOTHER US IF *WE* DON'T BOTHER *IT!* T'MORRA WE'LL HEAD ON INTO PORT BARRIOS AN' GET AN ASSAY ON OUR GOLD STRIKE.

OKAY, BILL-- WE HIT IT RICH THERE IN THAT STREAM! I *KNOW* WE DID!

THE OLD FOOL DON'T KNOW IT, BUT THIS IS HIS LAST NIGHT ON EARTH...HE *REALLY* THINKS I'M GONNA SHARE THE STRIKE WITH HIM! THAT STREAM BED IS LOADED WITH GOLD--AND *I'M* THE ONE WHO'LL CASH IN ON IT—AND *ALONE!*

LATER...

HE'S ASLEEP. NOW'S THE TIME TO GET RID OF HIM!.. OH-OH! HERE COMES THAT MONSTER!.. MAYBE I CAN GET RID OF *HIM* TOO! IT'S WORTH THE CHANCE!

HAW! SO IT'S FIRE THAT YOU'RE AFRAID OF, EH! WELL, HERE'S MORE OF IT!

NED GOES INTO THE CABIN, THERE'S A BLOW, A MUFFLED CRY, AND ....

I'LL THROW HIM IN THE SWAMP! HE'LL SINK AND NOBODY'LL BE THE WISER! AND THEN THE STRIKE'LL BE MINE!

BUT UNKNOWN TO NED, A PAIR OF GLEAMING EYES WATCH HIM WITH BURNING HATRED...

GOODBYE, BILL! YOU SHOULDA KNOWN BETTER THAN TO TRUST *ME!*

BOY! LOOK AT THIS DUST! AND THERE'S LOTS MORE WHERE THIS CAME FROM! I'LL BE RICH FOR THE REST OF MY LIFE! I'LL START INTO PORT BARRIOS TONIGHT SO I CAN BE THERE BY MORNING AND HAVE AN ASSAY MADE!

NED, HEADING FOR PORT BARRIOS, DOESN'T LOOK BEHIND HIM... IF HE DID, HE WOULD SEE THE HEAP PULLING BILL OUT OF THE SWAMP....

THE NEXT MORNING NED ARRIVES IN PORT BARRIOS... PORT BARRIOS... FILLED WITH LIFE, LAUGHTER... AND INTRIGUE!!!

HE GOES INTO A CANTINA....

SEE THIS GOLD DUST, BARTENDER? KEEP MY DRINKS COMIN' 'TIL IT'S ALL USED UP!

SI, SEÑOR!

JERRY! DIG THAT!

OH-OH! IT LOOKS LIKE JUNIOR HAS HIT PAY DIRT! HERE'S WHERE WE GO INTA ACTION, AL!

HEY, FRIEND! WE THOUGHT YOU SOUNDED LIKE A YANK! IT'S GOOD TA SEE SOMEBODY FROM BACK HOME!

I'M A YANK ALRIGHT! ...I'LL BET I'M THE RICHEST YANK IN THESE PARTS!

WELL, AIN'T THAT NICE! I THINK WE'RE GONNA DO BUSINESS TOGETHER, FRIEND!

IN FACT, MAYBE IT'S A GOOD IDEA IF WE STEP OUTSIDE RIGHT·NOW AN' DO A LITTLE TALKIN'! AL AN'ME GOT *LOTSA* THOUGHTS ABOUT GOLD DUST!

ULP!! A-A GUN!

IN YA GO, LITTLE MAN! RIGHT INTA THE BACK SEAT!

W-WHERE ARE YOU TAKIN' ME?

FOR A SHORT RIDE -- WHERE WE WON'T BE DISTURBED!

OKAY, JERRY! SEE IF HE'S READY TO TALK!

WE WANT TO KNOW WHERE YA GOT THE GOLD! AND HERE'S SOMETHING TA SHOW WE MEAN BUSINESS!

OWWWWW! S-SOMEONE GAVE THE DUST TO ME! THEY OWED ME MONEY!

LOOK, PUNK! DON'T PLAY GAMES WITH US! SEE THIS FIST? IT'S GONNA COME AT YOU 'TIL YA TELL US WHERE YOUR GOLD STAKE IS! IF YA DON'T TALK I MIGHT GET TIRED OF USIN' MY *FIST* AND, USE A *GUN!*

REMEMBER, IF YOU GIVE US THE INFO' WE'LL PLAY IT EQUAL--SHARE AND SHARE ALIKE! OTHERWISE IT'S CURTAINS! WHAT DO YOU SAY?

O-OKAY! YOU GOT ME LICKED! THE STAKE AIN'T FAR FROM HERE--MAYBE FOUR-FIVE MILES IN THE JUNGLE!

STOP THE CAR, AL! JUNIOR. HERE IS GONNA DRAW US A NICE MAP SHOWIN' EXACTLY WHERE THE GOLD IS!

THAT SHOWS WHAT A SMART YOUNG FELLA HE IS!

LOOK AT THE BOY DRAW, AL! HE'S A REGULAR ARTIST!

YEAH! HE'S DRAWIN' A NICE PLAIN MAP FOR US TO FOLLOW!

OKAY! JUST LET ME HAVE CHARGE OF THE MAP NOW!

NOT SO FAST, JERRY! I'M TAKIN' THE MAP!

NOT ON YOUR LIFE, AL! YOU DOUBLE-CROSSED ME IN CHICAGO— AND I AIN'T TAKIN' NO CHANCES OF YOUR DOIN' THE SAME THING AGAIN! SO JUST KEEP BACK!

PULL A ROD ON ME, WILL YA!!....

I'LL..... AGGGHHHH...

I TOLD YA, AL! I TOLD YA TO KEEP BACK! NOW YA WON'T EVER DOUBLE-CROSS ME AGAIN!

BAM!

COME ON, YOU! ONE PHONEY MOVE AND I'LL LET YOU HAVE IT TOO!

I'M COMIN'! DON'T SHOOT!

BUT AS NED AND JERRY WALK AWAY, THE DYING AL WEAKLY LIFTS HIS GUN AND AIMS IT AT JERRY...

I'LL GET... THE... RAT... I'LL GET... 'IM ...

NOW YOU AN' ME CAN G.......AGGGHHHHH....

WHAT TH'...!!

BAM!

THEY'VE KILLED EACH OTHER!—NOW I'LL JUST TAKE JERRY'S GUN AND GO BACK AND MAKE SURE *AL* IS POLISHED OFF.!--THAT WAS A CLOSE CALL FOR ME WITH THESE RATS!

HE'S GONE OKAY! SAVES ME THE TROUBLE! *NOW*, ONLY *I* KNOW ABOUT THE GOLD!

NOT THAT THEY WOULD EVER HAVE *FOUND* IT! THE MAP I DREW WOULD HAVE TAKEN THEM STRAIGHT INTO THE *SWAMP*! NOW TO GET BACK TO THE CABIN!

THE NEXT MORNING ...

BOY, I SURE PLAYED THIS CRAFTY! I'LL GO BACK TO THE STRIKE, PAN OUT A LOAD OF GOLD, AND LIVE LIKE A KING IN PORT BARRIOS...WHENEVER I NEED MORE DOUGH, I'LL COME BACK HERE AND GET ANOTHER LOAD!

LOOK AT THIS WONDERFUL YELLA STUFF...IT'S MINE... ALL MINE! NOBODY WILL EVER KNOW ABOUT THIS STRIKE BUT ME!

BUT SUDDENLY NED HEARS A FAMILIAR VOICE....

AIN'T YOU FORGETTIN' SOMEONE, NED?

HUH?

I GUESS I'M SURPRISIN' YOU SOME, EH, NED?

BILL??? BUT...I...I PUT YOU IN THE SWAMP ———— DEAD!

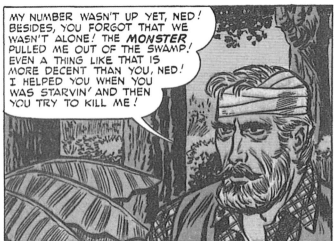

MY NUMBER WASN'T UP YET, NED! BESIDES, YOU FORGOT THAT WE WASN'T ALONE! THE *MONSTER* PULLED ME OUT OF THE SWAMP! EVEN A THING LIKE THAT IS MORE DECENT THAN YOU, NED! I HELPED YOU WHEN YOU WAS STARVIN' AND THEN YOU TRY TO KILL ME!

NO! YOU CAN'T BE ALIVE!... GET AWAY FROM ME!

YOU FOOL! I'M NO GHOST!

I'M GOIN' NUTS! BILL'S DEAD! HE *HAS* TO BE! NOTHIN' COULDA SAVED HIM FROM THAT SWAMP!

AS NED RACES INTO THE JUNGLE, THE HEAP STEPS OUT OF THE TALL GRASS...

WHAT CAN I DO...YIII! ...IT'S THE *MONSTER!*

215

SLOWLY, PONDEROUSLY, THE HEAP SHUFFLES
TOWARD THE CRINGING MAN...

HE'S... HE'S
COMIN' AT ME...

THESE BULLETS
WILL STOP HIM...

BUT NED FIRES BULLET AFTER BULLET INTO THE
MASSIVE CREATURE AND STILL THE HEAP KEEPS
COMING TOWARD HIM ....

I CAN'T STOP
HIM!... HELP!
HELP!

NED! NED! HE'S
HEADIN' YOU
INTA THE
SWAMP!

THE HEAP BACKS THE TERRIFIED MAN INTO
THE BOTTOMLESS MIRE.....

I'M TRAPPED!
HELP! HELP!

THERE'S NO WAY I
CAN SAVE HIM! BUT
THAT'S THE WAY HE
WANTED ME TO DIE!

THE HEAP DISAPPEARS INTO THE THICK JUNGLE...

NED GOT WHAT HE
DESERVED! EVEN THE
MONSTER SEEMS SATISFIED!
I WONDER WHAT HE IS –
AND WHERE HE CAME
FROM!....

216

THE HEAP

BOMBAY...A CITY OF TEEMING HUMANITY... WHERE ANY DOORWAY MIGHT BE THE AVENUE TO INTRIGUE ... WHERE A THOUSAND FANTASIES WALK ALONG IN LOIN CLOTHS... AND WHERE WE NOW SEE TWO TOURISTS, A MAN AND WOMAN, AS THEY APPROACH A POOR BEGGAR IN THE STREET....

ALMS! ALMS!

HERE YOU ARE, OLD MAN!

THIS WRETCHED ONE THANKS YOU, SAHIB!

JOHN, THEY SAY THAT THESE BEGGARS TELL THE MOST FASCINATING STORIES! GO ON--HAVE HIM TELL US ONE!

GLADLY, SAHIB! GLADLY WILL I TELL YOU A TALE...A TALE OF ONE OF NATURE'S STRANGEST CREATIONS...IS IT WORTH ANOTHER COPPER TO HEAR OF A THING THAT WAS ONCE A MAN... AND IS NOW LIKE A TREE?

OKAY-- HERE'S YOUR COPPER-- GO AHEAD!

THANK YOU, SAHIB... THANK YOU!...AND NOW FOR YOUR TALE...

SOME TIME AGO WHEN THE WHOLE WORLD WAS ENGAGED IN WARFARE, AN EVIL MAN OF THE SKIES, BARON VON EMMELMAN, WAS SHOT DOWN INTO A SWAMP AND SHOULD HAVE DIED—BUT NATURE PLAYED A PRANK AND DECIDED INSTEAD THAT SHE'D UNITE HIS HALF-DEAD BODY WITH HER OWN MYSTERIES AND SEND HIM ABOUT THE EARTH AS A CREATURE OF GOOD—A CREATURE THAT IS CALLED *THE HEAP*—AND ONE THAT WILL DEAL WITH ALL EVIL AS IT SEES FIT....

"AND SO IT HAPPENED THAT AT THE END OF THE GREAT STRUGGLE, THOSE WHO BROUGHT IT ABOUT SHOULD BE BROUGHT TO JUSTICE ... THEY WERE SOON ALL ROUNDED UP TO PAY FOR THEIR CRIMES...THAT IS, ALL BUT *ONE*".

"THIS ONE WAS KNOWN ONLY AS Q-4! THERE WERE NO PICTURES OF THIS MONSTER...NO WAY OF IDENTIFYING HIM! MANY TIMES JUST AS THE POLICE WERE ABOUT TO POUNCE ON HIM, THEY WOULD ARRIVE ONLY TO FIND THAT HE HAD DISAPPEARED AGAIN!!"

GENTLEMEN! SORRY I CAN'T WAIT FOR YOUR VISIT! I HAVE IMPORTANT BUSINESS ELSEWHERE! Q-4

"A REPORT WAS SOON SENT TO THE AUTHORITIES IN SOUTH AMERICA THAT Q-4 WAS ON HIS WAY TO THAT COUNTRY... SOON ALL RAILROADS, AIRPLANES AND STEAMSHIP LINES WERE CHECKED...PASSPORTS INSPECTED AND BAGGAGE SEARCHED FOR SOME CLUE ... ALL TO NO AVAIL!"

"UNTIL ONE DAY IN THE SLEEPY VILLAGE OF SAN PABLO, ARGENTINA ..."

MADRÉ MIO!

SWISH

INSPECTOR!.. INSPECTOR!

YES, JUAN! WHAT IS IT? WHAT'S WRONG?

THEES NOTE... SHE CAME THROUGH THE WINDOW ON THEES KNIFE!..

CALM YOURSELF, JUAN! HAND ME THE NOTE!

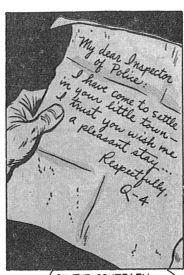

My dear Inspector of Police:
I have come to settle in your little town — I trust you wish me a pleasant stay...
Respectfully,
Q-4

WHAT'S THE TROUBLE, INSPECTOR? YOU LOOK DISTURBED!

I AM, CAPTAIN MORGAN! THE MAN YOU ARE SEARCHING FOR HAS COME TO THIS TOWN!... HE HAS SENT ME A NOTE TELLING ME SO!

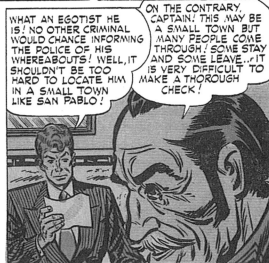

WHAT AN EGOTIST HE IS! NO OTHER CRIMINAL WOULD CHANCE INFORMING THE POLICE OF HIS WHEREABOUTS! WELL, IT SHOULDN'T BE TOO HARD TO LOCATE HIM IN A SMALL TOWN LIKE SAN PABLO!

ON THE CONTRARY, CAPTAIN! THIS MAY BE A SMALL TOWN BUT MANY PEOPLE COME THROUGH! SOME STAY AND SOME LEAVE...IT IS VERY DIFFICULT TO MAKE A THOROUGH CHECK!

WELL, IS THERE ANYONE IN TOWN THAT MIGHT GIVE ME A LEAD ON HIM?

THERE ARE TWO PEOPLE WHO MIGHT BE OF SOME HELP!

WHO ARE THEY?

ONE IS SEÑOR MATTICK, A REFUGEE FROM EUROPE! HE MIGHT KNOW SOMETHING OF Q-4! HE KEEPS TO HIMSELF QUITE A BIT BUT HAS DONE NOTHING TO CAST SUSPICION HIS WAY!

WHO'S THE OTHER?

SEÑORA MARIA VALDEZ! SHE IS IN THE CLEAR.. I KNEW HER FATHER BEFORE HE DIED! THE SEÑORA CAME BACK HOME TO TAKE OVER HER FATHER'S ESTATE! SHE MAY BE OF SOME HELP, FOR SHE SPENT MANY YEARS IN EUROPE DURING THE WAR!...

HOW CAN SHE HELP ME?

SHE HAS MANY FRIENDS IN EUROPE WHO KEEP HER INFORMED!.. BESIDES I THINK SHE'D *LIKE* TO HELP YOU AS MUCH AS SHE POSSIBLY CAN!

WHY?

BECAUSE HER HUSBAND WAS *KILLED* BY Q-4!

LATER AS CAPTAIN MORGAN IS ON HIS WAY TO SEE SEÑOR MATTICK...

IMAGINE A WHOLESALE KILLER LIKE Q-4 LOOSE IN A SLEEPY LITTLE BURG LIKE THIS... I WONDER WHY HE CAME HERE!.. I'VE GOT A HUNCH THAT IF I DON'T GET HIM BEFORE HE LEAVES SAN PABLO, I'LL NEVER GET HIM! AH, THERE'S MATTICK'S PLACE NOW!

I'D LIKE TO SEE SEÑOR MATTICK, PLEASE!

OF COURSE! COME IN, SEÑOR!

MATTICK CERTAINLY HAS A COMFY LITTLE LAYOUT HERE!

SEÑOR MATTICK?

YES, SEÑOR! WHAT CAN I DO FOR YOU?

I'VE BEEN SENT BY THE GOVERNMENT TO CHECK ON ALL NON-RESIDENTS OF THIS TOWN.! I WOULD LIKE TO SEE YOUR PASSPORT AND OTHER CREDENTIALS!

MOST CERTAINLY, SEÑOR! BUT YOU NEEDN'T TRY TO CONCEAL THE FACT THAT YOU ARE A REPRESENTATIVE OF THE WAR CRIMES COMMISSION!

HOW DID YOU KNOW THAT?

EVERYONE KNOWS! REMEMBER, SEÑOR, THAT SAN PABLO IS A SMALL TOWN... NEWS TRAVELS FAST! DO YOU REALLY THINK THAT YOU CAN FIND A CLEVER MAN LIKE Q-4?

I *KNOW* I CAN, SEÑOR MATTICK! YOUR CREDENTIALS SEEM TO BE IN ORDER, ALTHOUGH I'M SURE THAT ANY INFORMATION THAT I *WANT* YOU *WON'T* GIVE ME! I'LL BE BACK SOONER THAN YOU EXPECT!

I'LL ALWAYS BE EXPECTING YOU, SEÑOR!

THAT MATTICK CHARACTER ACTED SO SUSPICIOUS HE MAY BE INNOCENT! I'D BETTER DROP IN ON SEÑORA VALDEZ, MAYBE I CAN LEARN SOMETHING THERE!

WHO IS IT, JOSE?

A CAPTAIN MORGAN, SEÑORA VALDEZ!

SHOW THE GENTLEMAN IN, JOSE!

THEES WAY, CAPTAIN!

THANKS!

COME SIT BY THE FIRE, CAPTAIN! YOU MUST BE SOAKED! SOME BRANDY, JOSE!

THANK YOU, SEÑORA!

SEÑORA VALDEZ, I'M FROM THE WAR CRIMES COMMISSION! WE'RE TRYING TO TRACK DOWN ONE OF THE WORST CRIMINALS OF THE WAR... THE MAN WHO KILLED YOUR HUSBAND...

Q-4!? IS HE HERE?

YES! I'M SORRY TO CAUSE YOU PAIN, SEÑORA, BUT IN ORDER TO CATCH THIS MAN WE MUST HAVE MORE INFORMATION ABOUT HIM!..

FORGIVE ME, CAPTAIN! PLEASE GO ON...I'LL DO ANYTHING I CAN TO HELP!

I WANT YOU TO CONTACT ALL THE PEOPLE YOU KNEW IN EUROPE ...GET EVERY SCRAP OF INFORMATION ABOUT Q-4 YOU CAN! ANYTHING AT ALL!

I WILL, CAPTAIN MORGAN, AND I'LL GET IN TOUCH WITH YOU AS SOON AS I LEARN ANYTHING!

I HOPE, CAPTAIN, THAT ALL YOUR VISITS WON'T BE BUSINESS!..

BELIEVE ME, SEÑORA, THEY WON'T BE!

AFTER CAPTAIN MORGAN LEAVES...

WHAT'S WRONG WITH YOU, JOSE? YOU'RE FIDGETING LIKE AN OLD WOMAN!

I DON'T LIKE THE WAY THINGS ARE GOING! I NEVER DID APPROVE OF *YOUR* SENDING THAT NOTE TO THE POLICE INSPECTOR... THEY'LL FIND OUT! I KNOW IT!

SO YOU'RE AFRAID THEY'LL FIND OUT THAT *I'M* Q-4, EH, JOSE? THAT NOTE WAS JUST TO SHOW THEM HOW EASY IT IS FOR ME TO SLIP FROM THEIR GRASP!

WELL! HOW LONG MUST WE STAY IN THIS ACCURSED PLACE?

JUST UNTIL WE HEAR THAT THE BOAT IS READY TO SAIL!

THAT GOLD IS CURSED! I FEEL IT!

DON'T BE A CHILD, JOSE! WE NEED MONEY WHEREVER WE GO... I HAD IT BURIED HERE FOR SUCH A PURPOSE! ALL WE DO IS DIG IT UP AT THE OLD TEMPLE AND MEET THE BOAT AT THE APPOINTED TIME! AND THEN...

WE'LL GO TO THE UNITED STATES, FREE AS BIRDS, WITH NOTHING TO DO BUT SPEND MONEY!

YOU FORGET, *HE* KNEW WHO YOU WERE... *HE* WAS THE ONLY ONE WHO KNEW...

VON EMMELMAN IS DEAD, JOSE! I KNOW FOR CERTAIN THAT HE'S DEAD! I READ THE REPORT OF HIS DEATH.. I WENT TO THE SCENE OF THE CRASH.. I SAW HIS BODY! HE WAS THE ONLY LIVING SOUL BESIDE *YOU* WHO KNEW WHO I AM... BUT HE'S DEAD...DO YOU HEAR.. *DEAD!*

WHILE OUTSIDE THE WINDOW *THE BURNING EYES OF THE HEAP* WATCH THE WOMAN INSIDE ---

"IT WASN'T LONG AFTER THAT CAPTAIN MORGAN BECAME A CONSTANT VISITOR AT THE HOME OF SEÑORA VALDEZ..."

MARIA, I WANT TO MARRY YOU AND TAKE YOU HOME WITH ME!

GIVE ME A FEW DAYS TO THINK IT OVER, BOB!

LATER...

HE'S GONE! WHY DO YOU KEEP HIM?... HE MAY GET SUSPICIOUS!

DON'T BE STUPID, JOSE! HE'S A SPLENDID COVER-UP FOR US! BESIDES, I WANT TO SEE HIS FACE WHEN HE FINDS OUT WHO I AM!

THE MESSAGE HAS COME FROM THE BOAT CAPTAIN! WE'RE TO MEET THEM AT A COVE TWO MILES FROM THE TEMPLE AT EXACTLY 4:30 A.M. -THEY WON'T WAIT A MINUTE AFTER THE APPOINTED TIME!

WE'LL BE THERE! CALL MORGAN AND TELL HIM TO COME AT ONCE... TELL HIM THAT I'VE RECEIVED A THREATENING LETTER FROM Q-4! THAT'LL BRING HIM ON THE RUN!

SOON AFTER...

I CAME AS SOON AS I GOT YOUR CALL, MARIA!

THE NOTE HE SENT ME TOLD ME TO COME TO THE OLD TEMPLE IN THE JUNGLE! I WANT YOU TO COME WITH ME! HIS CAPTURE WOULD MAKE YOU FAMOUS! BUT CALL THE POLICE AND TELL THEM TO COME TWO HOURS AFTER WE LEAVE IN CASE ANYTHING SHOULD GO WRONG!

AN HOUR LATER...

WE SHOULD BE AT THE TEMPLE ANY MINUTE NOW!

THERE IT IS!

JOSE! YOU GO AND DIG UP THE GOLD! I WILL TAKE CARE OF CAPTAIN MORGAN!

MARIA! WHAT IS THIS?? ARE YOU MAD???

A FEW MINUTES LATER...

I'VE GOT THE GOLD, MARIA! LET'S BE ON OUR WAY! DID YOU KILL THE FOOL?

NO! I JUST KNOCKED HIM UNCONSCIOUS WITH THE GUN! WHEN THE POLICE ARRIVE THEY'LL FIND THIS NOTE PINNED ON HIM, TELLING WHO I AM! I'LL MAKE COMPLETE FOOLS OF THEM ALL! MEANWHILE WE'LL MAKE OUR ESCAPE EASILY!

"AS MARIA AND JOSE MAKE THEIR DASH THROUGH THE WOODS, ANOTHER FIGURE LUMBERS OUT OF THE JUNGLE AND MOVES SLOWLY BEHIND THEM... THE HEAP BEGINS TO STALK HIS PREY...."

SOON...

JOSE! LOOK! WHAT IS IT?

I-I DON'T KNOW! BULLETS DON'T HARM IT! QUICKLY! COME THIS WAY! WE MAY GET AWAY FROM IT!

THE
HEAP

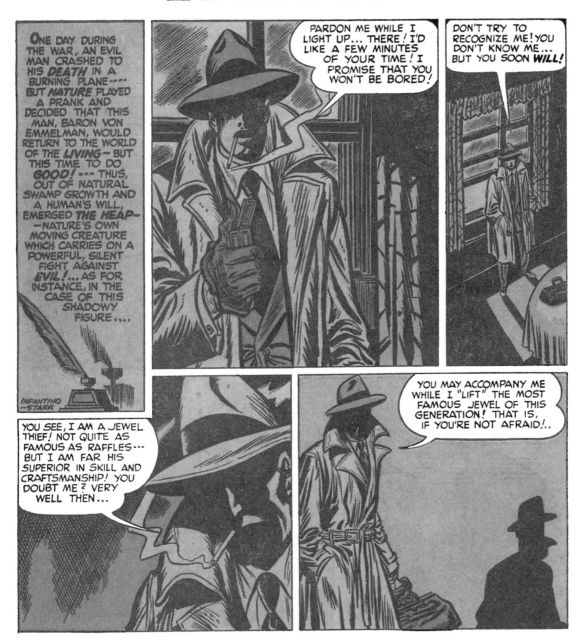

TAXI!!

SO AS NOT TO WASTE TIME, I SHALL UTILIZE THE NEXT FIFTEEN MINUTES BY INFORMING YOU FURTHER OF THE ORIGIN OF THIS JEWEL! IT WILL TAKE US THAT LONG TO ARRIVE AT OUR DESTINATION! ..... ABOUT THIRTY YEARS AGO, 3 OF THE WORLD'S MOST NOTORIOUS JEWEL THIEVES MET IN A LONELY WATERFRONT WAREHOUSE...

ENTER QUICKLY! WE HAVE LITTLE TIME!

THEN WE ARE ALL IN AGREEMENT, GENTLEMEN! WE SHALL HAVE THIS MOST FABULOUS JEWEL SET INTO A NECK BAND BY AN EXPERT CRAFTSMAN! .. THEN WE SHALL SECRETE IT IN SUCH A PLACE, WITH SO MANY TRICKY OBSTACLES BEFORE IT, THAT ITS THEFT WILL BE ALMOST IMPOSSIBLE .....

THEN, AFTER OUR DEATHS, KNOWLEDGE OF THE EXISTENCE OF THIS BAND SHALL BE MADE PUBLIC...AND THE ONE WHO CAN STEAL IT SHALL WIN THE TITLE OF *MASTER JEWEL THIEF!!*

NOW YOU UNDERSTAND EXACTLY WHAT WE WANT, M'SIEU STONER!!

REST ASSURED, GENTLEMEN, THE VON EMMELMAN JEWEL WILL HAVE A SETTING WORTHY OF ITS VALUE!

AND NOT LONG AFTER...

YES! THE NECK BAND IS FINISHED, GENTLEMEN!

WELL, GET IT! *GET IT!!*

PERFECT, STONER! IN FACT... *EXCELLENT!*

SO SORRY, STONER... BUT EVEN *YOU* MUSTN'T KNOW! *THIS* IS THE ONLY WAY!

OH, YES! THEY KILLED STONER! AND SOON AFTER, THEY TOO WERE GONE! BUT THAT'S ONLY AS IT SHOULD BE! MANY TRIED TO STEAL THE NECK BAND BUT THEY ALL FAILED! BUT I... HA! HA! I PLANNED TOO WELL! I SHALL SUCCEED!

THIS IS IT, DRIVER! PULL UP HERE!

SINCE MY METHODS MUST REMAIN MY OWN SECRET, I SHALL LEAVE YOU HERE FOR A FEW MOMENTS! I SHALL RETURN SHORTLY!

AND SOON...

SEE HOW SIMPLE IT WAS! AND THERE WASN'T EVEN THE SLIGHTEST SUSPICION... I'VE BEEN PLANNING THIS FOR TOO LONG!

MINUTES LATER...

AH! WE ARE COMPLETELY OUT OF DANGER NOW! YOU HAVE INDEED WITNESSED A HISTORICAL EVENT!

BUT NOW, I MUST DISPOSE OF THIS MOST VALUABLE PIECE! AND IN DOING SO WEALTH AND FAME SHALL BE MINE!

SOMETIME LATER...IN THE BACK ROOM OF A CURIO SHOP...

MMM! MM..HMMM! I ADMIRE YOUR COURAGE, SIR...BUT I DON'T ENVY YOU!

WHAT'S WRONG? IT'S THE AUTHENTIC PIECE, ISN'T IT?

OH, **THAT** I DON'T DOUBT! BUT DON'T YOU REALIZE THAT BOTH THE POLICE AND THE UNDERWORLD ARE AFTER THE POSSESSOR OF THIS OBJECT? IT'S WORTH EASILY ALL OF TWO MILLION DOLLARS... BUT IT'S HOT! I MIGHT POSSIBLY CONSIDER A TRANSACTION IN ABOUT TWO YEARS... IF YOU STILL HAVE IT!

HMM! TWO YEARS, EH?

THERE WON'T BE A CON MAN IN THE RACKETS WHO WON'T BE AFTER IT! LET'S SEE NOW!.. WAIT! YES! *THAT'S IT!!*

YOU ARE THE BEST LOCK AND KEY MAN IN THE COUNTRY, HUNTS! YOU MUST DO AS I ASK!!

IT'S AWFUL RISKY...BUT FOR $25,000...

YOU'RE A PIG, HUNTS... BUT I HAVE NO ALTERNATIVE! I WANT AN IMPREGNABLE LOCK ON THE BAND! IT WILL BE PLACED AROUND MY NECK AND A STRIP OF FALSE SKIN OVER TO HIDE IT! YOU SHALL HOLD THE KEY AS INSURANCE FOR THE $25,000!

AFTER A LABORIOUS TWO WEEKS...

THERE IT IS! IT'S PERFECT! NO ONE COULD EVER TELL YOU HAD IT ON!... AND I HAVE THE KEY!

YOU'RE A GENIUS, HUNTS...A GENIUS...

...AND A FOOL! YOU DIDN'T REALLY THINK I'D LET YOU KEEP THE KEY, DID YOU?

BAM! BAM!

THE KEY TO MY VERY LIFE...AND **MY FUTURE!**

LIKE MYSELF, HUNTS, YOU WERE AN ARTIST... A GENIUS! IT'S A PITY YOUR CAREER HAD TO COME TO SUCH AN ABRUPT HALT! BUT NO ONE MUST KNOW OF THE NECK BAND'S LOCATION!

NOW THIS KEY BECOMES AS VALUABLE AS THE BAND ITSELF! AND WHAT MORE SAFE PLACE CAN I FIND THAN IN A FOREST?

HA! HA! MY FUTURE IS INSURED! WHAT POSSIBLE OBSTACLE CAN STAND IN MY WAY NOW? HA! HA!

AH! THAT OLD TREE IN THE CLEARING! A PERFECT PLACE TO HIDE THE KEY!

IT'S ODD WHAT AN ALMOST COMIC HUMAN SHAPE THIS TREE HAS! WELL, DON'T WALK AWAY ON ME, OLD FELLOW! HA! HA! HA!

THE NEXT MORNING IN A CERTAIN DR. SELIG'S OFFICE ....

INSPECTOR BENET AND MR. SANDEE ARE HERE, DR. SELIG!

AH! RIGHT ON TIME! SEND THEM IN, MISS KANE!

FAMOUS JEWEL THIEVES OF HISTORY

GOOD MORNING, GENTLEMEN! AND HOW ARE MY FAVORITE POLICE INSPECTOR AND CRIMINOLOGIST FEELING?

FINE, SIR!

SWELL, DOC! AND YOURSELF?..

229

YOU'RE JOKING OF COURSE, DR. SELIG!

NO! NO! I SAY THAT IN ALL SERIOUSNESS!

BOTH OF YOU MEN HAVE HAD ACCESS TO THE BUILDING FROM WHICH THE NECKBAND WAS TAKEN!.... BOTH OF YOU HAD TIME TO STUDY EVERY NOOK AND CRANNY AND PASSAGEWAY.....

I'M NOT SURE WHETHER I SHOULD FEEL INSULTED OR CONSIDER MYSELF A GENIUS FOR BEING SUSPECTED!

I HOPE NEITHER! GOOD DAY, GENTLE-MEN!

A WEEK LATER...

THESE X-RAY REPORTS OF INSPECTOR BENET AND MR. SANDEE HAVE ARRIVED, DR. SELIG!

OH! GOOD! I'LL LOOK AT THEM NOW, MISS KANE!

GREAT SCOTT! MISS KANE! GET THIS PATIENT ON THE PHONE... *IMMEDIATELY!*

HELLO? OH, HELLO, DOCTOR! I JUST CAME IN! *WHAT?* IT SHOWED UP IN THE X-RAY??

EXACTLY! AND WHAT'S MORE, THE REPORT SHOWS THAT YOUR METABOLISM HAS SLOWED UP! IN OTHER WORDS, YOUR FOOD INTAKE IS TURNING MOSTLY TO FAT INSTEAD OF ENERGY! YOU'RE PUTTING ON WEIGHT BECAUSE OF IT *EVEN NOW!* THAT *BAND* WILL *CHOKE* YOU!!

HELLO? *SANDEE...* HELLO?...

THE KEY! I MUST GET THE KEY!.. GOT TO GET THIS THING OFF MY NECK!!

7

231

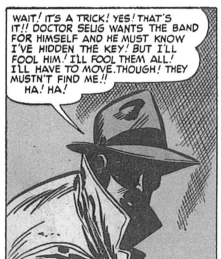

WAIT! IT'S A TRICK! YES! THAT'S IT!! DOCTOR SELIG WANTS THE BAND FOR HIMSELF AND HE MUST KNOW I'VE HIDDEN THE KEY! BUT I'LL FOOL HIM! I'LL FOOL THEM ALL! I'LL HAVE TO MOVE, THOUGH! THEY MUSTN'T FIND ME!! HA! HA!

THE FOLLOWING MONDAY...

HMMM! SEEMS KINDA STUFFY IN HERE! I'LL OPEN THE WINDOW!

ODD! I CAN'T SEEM TO GET ENOUGH AIR!

TUESDAY...

BLASTED CLEANERS! THIS SUIT WAS A PERFECT FIT BEFORE I SENT IT OUT TO BE CLEANED! NOW IT'S TIGHT!!

WEDNESDAY...

HMMM! WATCH STRAP DOESN'T FIT! MUST NEED AN ADJUSTMENT!

THURSDAY...

(PUFF)... FEELING TIRED AND SLUGGISH LATELY! DON'T KNOW WHY...

FRIDAY...

...COUGH...COUGH...MUST BE COMING DOWN WITH A COLD! ALL CHOKED UP! HARD TO BREATHE! COLLAR...TIGHT!

SATURDAY...

DOCTOR SELIG WASN'T KIDDING! I AM GETTING FAT! THAT'S IT!! THE TIGHT SUIT...SMALL WATCH STRAP... SLUGGISH FEELING!! I GOTTA GET THE KEY! I GOTTA GET THIS THING OFF!!...

THERE IT IS! THE OLD TREE WHERE I HID IT!... ...ALMOST THERE!/...

'THE TREE!..IT'S MOVING!! WAIT! WAIT!! THE KEY!! ..I'LL CHOKE!

STOP! STOP!.. PLEASE!/...

I...CAN'T... GO...ON...

THE KEY! GIVE ME THE KEY!!! GIVE ME THE KEY! GIVE ME THE KEY... GIVE ME THE KEY.....

LATER...

THAT'S THE WAY WE FOUND HIM, INSPECTOR... CHOKED TO DEATH BY THAT NECKLACE--AND THE KEY NEAR HIS HAND! WE CAN'T UNDERSTAND WHY HE DIDN'T USE IT!!

SO!.. IT WAS SANDEE! LET ME SEE THAT NECKLACE FOR WHICH HE GAVE HIS LIFE....

SOMETHING WRONG, INSPECTOR?

NO-NOTHING WRONG.. BUT IT'S EASY TO SEE WHY HE RISKED HIS LIFE TO GET THIS HUNK OF BEAUTY !! ....BUT PERSONALLY, I'D PREFER A PLAINER NECKTIE... AND ONE WITH A LITTLE MORE STRETCH !!

When you want to know a little more, Chamber of Chills Companion coming soon from PS Artbooks

Nah, four books devoted to Harvey's original title just wasn't enough . . .
so we've put together a whole new volume chock full to the rafters with special articles and
never-before-seen artwork and stories. Don't delay -- order your copy today: the print run will
be strictly limited so when they're gone . . . they're gone.

CHAMBER OF CHILLS COMPANION available from your local store . . .
but only if you tell 'em! Cover your back and order direct from either
www.psartbooks.com or **www.pspublishing.co.uk**

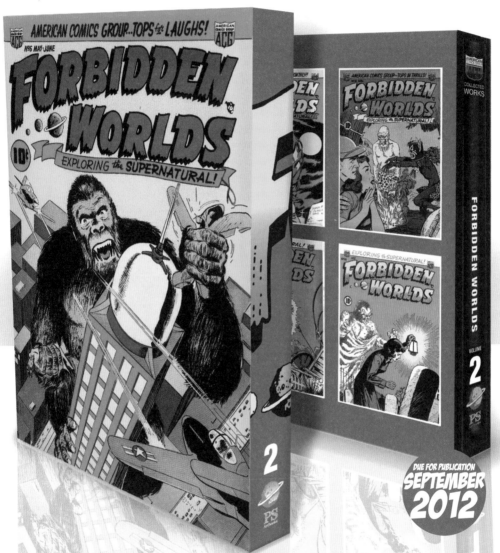

Introducing Planet Comics
exclusively from PS Artbooks

Hey, PS Artbooks is going all 'out of this furshlugginer world' with the first volume of the ground-breaking awe-filled Planet Comics that appeared from Fiction House over a thirteen-year period ending in 1953. They're all here . . . Flint Baker, Reef Ryan, The Space Rangers, Gale Allen, Star Pirate, Mysta of the Moon, Norge Benson plus many more AND a bevy of the most scantily-clad females you're likely to see outside of Silvio Dante's Bada Bing strip joint in The Sopranos.

PLANET COMICS VOLUME ONE 288 full color pages with a foil blocked leatherlook cover complete with dustjacket limited to just 1700 copies worldwide.
Also available is a slipcase version limited to just 300, available from your local store . . . but only if you tell 'em! Better still, cover your back and order direct from either
www.psartbooks.com or www.pspublishing.co.uk

240